"WE'VE LOST PRIMARY POWER IN OPS," NGUYEN SAID.

"Auxiliaries have kicked in, but most of our systems are down."

"Can you get the primaries back up?" Lenaris asked.

"Trying," Nguyen said. "It looks like an override from somewhere . . ." He tapped different sequences into his control interface, then slammed his hands on the console in frustration. "I'm locked out. We no longer have control of the station."

"Then who does?" Akaar demanded.

An electronic hum from the transporter stage gave him his answer. A figure materialized and took a single step forward, phaser in hand, surveying the operations center with a glare that, Lenaris thought, could melt neutronium.

Ro Laren.

STAR TREK
DEEP SPACE NINE®

MISSION: GAMMA

BOOK FOUR OF FOUR

LESSER EVIL

ROBERT SIMPSON

Based upon STAR TREK®
created by Gene Roddenberry, and
STAR TREK: DEEP SPACE NINE
created by Rick Berman & Michael Piller

POCKET BOOKS
New York   London   Toronto   Sydney   Singapore   Kora II

An *Original* Publication of POCKET BOOKS

POCKET BOOKS, a division of Simon & Schuster, Inc.
1230 Avenue of the Americas, New York, NY 10020

STAR TREK is a Registered Trademark of Paramount Pictures.

This book is published by Pocket Books, a division of Simon & Schuster, Inc., under exclusive license from Paramount Pictures.

ISBN: 0-7434-1024-6

First Pocket Books printing November 2002

10 9 8 7 6 5 4 3 2 1

POCKET and colophon are registered trademarks of Simon & Schuster, Inc.

For information regarding special discounts for bulk purchases, please contact Simon & Schuster Special Sales at 1-800-456-6798 or business@simonandschuster.com

Cover art by Cliff Nielsen

Printed in the U.S.A.

It may be that the gulfs will wash us down:
It may be we shall touch the Happy Isles,
And see the great Achilles, whom we knew.
Tho' much is taken, much abides; and tho'
We are not now that strength which in old days
Moved earth and heaven; that which we are, we are;
One equal temper of heroic hearts,
Made weak by time and fate, but strong in will
To strive, to seek, to find, and not to yield.

—ALFRED, LORD TENNYSON,
"ULYSSES"

PROLOGUE

Smells were not, contrary to what most people believed, the most memorable things about kitchens. What stayed with a person, long after an aroma had faded, were the sounds. The clatter of pans, the crackle and snapping bubbles of oil boiling, the crisp, loud crunching snap of fresh vegetables cut on a worn chopping board, or of a stolen stem of celery chewed while a salad is prepared. Voices, laughing. It was, thought Judith Sisko, symphonic. It spoke to heart, and to soul, and it told a tale.

As she stood at the foot of the stairs that led up to the family rooms above Sisko's Creole Kitchen and thought back over the most vivid memories of her childhood, it was the sounds coming from the kitchen Judith remembered most vividly. Life centered around that place, not just because her father was a chef or that

1

he ran the restaurant below their home, but because the kitchen was the place that everyone gathered to share news, and where her father somehow, no matter what the news was, always seemed able to make the worst moments feel happy.

Sounds of life.

So it was with a great sense of loss that she stood there now, in the place where she'd grown up, to find it utterly, desolately silent. The restaurant had been closed for weeks now. Where once Humans, Bolians, Vulcans, and a half-dozen other species had all eaten casually in the main dining area at any given time . . . now a fine layer of dust covered the bare wooden tables.

"Can I fix you some breakfast?" a voice said, snapping Judith back.

"Thanks, Gaby, but I'll pass," she said. Gabrielle Vicente was perhaps the only other constant for Judith at the restaurant. She almost always looked as she did now, dressed in a neatly pressed white shirt and pants. The only thing missing was her apron, which was invariably stained with okra and olive oil.

Gaby walked past Judith on her way to the garden, placing a reassuring hand on her shoulder. "Let me know if there's anything I can do," she said. "I was going to head home after I tended to the vegetables, but if you need me to stay—"

Judith smiled weakly and shook her head. "No, go home. You deserve to rest. I'll be fine."

"You're sure?"

Judith nodded.

"I'm just a call away if you need anything, any-time," Gaby insisted.

"I know. Thanks." They hugged, and Gaby pro-ceeded out back.

Judith's gaze followed the stairs up to the second floor. There was no putting this off. Her hand took hold of the great post that anchored the smooth wooden banister, and she started her ascent.

Walking down the hallway next to the stairwell, Judith stopped at the closed door of the master bed-room, her hand hovering over the knob. She released a breath and opened the door.

Sitting at the window overlooking the garden was her father.

The first thing she noticed was how stooped his shoulders were. Sitting or standing, Dad always had his head held high, shoulders back, as if daring the world to push against him. Ramrod straight and facing whatever came his way, that's what she remembered. His hair, always salt-and-peppered from the earliest images she had of him, was more white now than any-thing else, and the side of his face seemed tight, drawn. His arms had become so thin they practically disap-peared in the sleeve of his loose-fitting shirt. She knew he'd been losing weight and wearing his age even be-fore his collapse. He sat forward with his large, gnarled hands pressed together between his knees, looking out the window, like a caged bird who misses the sky.

"Dad?" she said when the standing and staring was too much to keep doing. He didn't answer, so she said it again.

"The Crenshaws aren't going to make it this season," Joseph Sisko said without turning. "Some kind of grubs been chewing at the roots. Gaby tries hard, but she can't stay ahead of them."

"Grubs need to eat, too," she said.

Dad nodded. "I suppose it doesn't really matter."

Then Judith heard something she hadn't since she arrived from Portland a few days earlier—a laugh. Slight, but it was there.

"Nice to hear you laugh."

"It's just strange not to hear someone nag at me about getting out of this room."

"I would if I thought it'd do any good. But you've always known your own mind."

"Finally, one of my children shows some sense," Dad said.

"You're still thinking about Ben, aren't you?" Judith asked. She'd hesitated mentioning her brother's name before now, dancing around it whenever possible, but it was clear that she wasn't going to be able not to mention him forever.

Dad continued looking out the window. Several minutes passed before he spoke again. "You know, I've always worked that garden with my hands, from before you were born. With all the technology in the world—and believe me, I appreciate it all, in its place—that was the one place where nothing aside from water, sunshine, and time could make a difference. When Ben was a little boy, he used to go out there and wiggle his toes in the dirt. You, too, as I recall. It never seemed like those days would end."

"Ben knew the risks that came with his job, Dad," Judith said gently. "We all did. The day he left for Starfleet Academy, we knew we might have to deal with the possibility that he'd never come home."

"Don't talk to me about risks," Dad snapped. "He wasn't killed by the Tzenkethi or vaporized by the Borg or blown to hell by the Dominion. Even that I could accept. I could make peace with it and move on. But he was taken from us, Judith. That damn planet and those so-called prophets took him away from everything he loves, and everyone that loves him. And still they weren't satisfied. They had to take my grandson, too."

"We don't know that, Dad. What happened to Jake, wherever he is, it may have nothing to do with Ben.

He scowled at her. "Maybe you can convince yourself of that. I can't. The boy's ship disappears the moment it leaves for Earth, and you want me to believe it has nothing to do with that damned thing . . . that wormhole?

Her father shook his head, muttering, "I told him not to take that assignment. Seven years ago, I told him. Stay on Mars, I said. Build ships. At least you'll be close to Earth. Or forget Starfleet and just come home. He wasn't over Jen's death. He needed more time. But he went anyway, and what's worse is that he took Jake with him to that floating junkyard. Now they're both gone." He buried his face in his hands. "God forgive me, sometimes I wish Ben had never been born."

"Dad, you don't mean that—"

"Sometimes I do," he confessed, eyes welling with tears as he spoke. "I know I shouldn't, but I can't help it. They did it, Judith. They made him. Used me and Sarah both just so we'd bring Ben into the world, so that years later they could use *him*. Like they used me. Like they've used all of us."

Judith took her father's head in her hands and pulled him close as he wept. He seemed so much smaller now, so diminished.

She recalled when her father had come to see her in Portland over a year ago—an unprecedented visit—just so he could try to explain the bizarre story he needed to share. How her late mother Rebecca had actually been Dad's second wife, and not Ben's mother at all. How Ben had learned the truth, that his birth mother Sarah had been the vessel for one of the alien entities who supposedly lived in the Bajoran wormhole, just so that Ben could be born to fulfill his destiny on the other side of the quadrant. It seemed impossible, even in a universe already teeming with unlikely wonders. Judith had not been sure she could believe it. But as her father told her his tale, she knew that *he* did.

Ah, Ben . . . How do I make sense of this? To her, Benjamin Lafayette Sisko was nothing more or less than her gawky older brother: adorable as a child, infuriating as a teenager, a source of pride as a man. But there was nothing supernatural about him. He was the obnoxious brat who pushed her into the creek when she was nine. He was the mechanical genius who helped her construct their robotic skeleton float for that last Mardi Gras before he enrolled in the Academy, then blamed her when it fell drunkenly against the ornate wrought-iron railing on one of the balconies that lined Bourbon Street. (She never did get him to admit that he'd overloaded the servos, causing the float to veer off course as it walked.) And he was the awkward Starfleet ensign introducing his fiancée to the family for the first time. Judith remembered thinking she'd never seen a man so nervous as when Dad launched into stories of Ben's mischievous youth . . . or a man more in love as Ben kissed the heads of Jennifer and their nursing newborn son the morning after Jake was born.

When Jennifer died . . . Judith had known it was a wound from which Ben would never completely recover; it had been too brutal, and too closely tied to his life as a Starfleet officer for him not to believe he bore some responsibility for her death. After his reassignment to Utopia Planitia following a brief stint supervising construction of habitats in orbit of Earth, Judith made a point to visit him and Jake during her annual tour with the Martian Philharmonic. He'd been so distant, and she worried that the old connection between them was lost forever, as so much else had been lost when Jennifer died. But then after Jake had turned in, he came out to see her on his apartment's observation deck, and as they both stood watching the red planet rotate overhead, he started talking.

"I've been reassigned," he began.

She looked at him, knowing from the way he'd said it that he hadn't meant he was going back to Earth. "Where are you headed?" she'd asked.

"Bajor," he'd said.

"I don't think I know it."

"No reason you should," Ben told her. *"It's a Cardassian subject world. The Cardassians are withdrawing after fifty years of occupation. Now the Bajorans have petitioned the Federation for membership and invited Starfleet to help them administrate a space station the Cardassians are abandoning, for use as a Federation starbase."*

"Cardassia . . ." Judith had repeated. *That was a name she'd recognized. Ben's new assignment would be taking him to the fringes of Federation space.*

"I'm to be the station commander," Ben elaborated. *"Starfleet needs someone to work with the Bajorans, help prepare them for entry into the Federation. They're promoting me to full commander for the job."*

"Why you?" Judith had asked.

Ben had smiled grimly as he watched Olympus Mons come into view. *"I've been asking myself the same question. I suspect one reason is all those years working with Curzon. They have this misplaced idea I've learned the fine art of diplomacy."*

Judith had decided to ignore Ben's modesty. *"Is there another reason?"*

Ben sighed, then turned his gaze toward an EVA crew working on the hull of a nearby starship nestled inside the surrounding lattice of a repair scaffold. *"I think they feel I've been back in drydock long enough."*

"Have you told Dad yet?"

Ben shook his head.

"When do you leave?"

He met her eyes for the first time that evening. "Jake and I ship out in three days."

"Three days?" she'd cried. "Were you even going to tell me if I hadn't come to Mars? Ben, what the hell are you waiting for? How can you spring this on Dad with only three days' notice?"

"The orders came through yesterday," Ben had explained. "I was planning to take a shuttle to Earth tomorrow."

"He won't be happy about this, you know."

"I know. But he'll get over it . . ." Ben must have seen how angry that response had made her, because he added quickly, ". . . because chances are the assignment won't last, anyway. Nothing I've heard about the political situation on Bajor makes me optimistic about their readiness. And . . . I've been giving serious thought to resigning, coming back to Earth."

Judith frowned. "Let me get this straight. You're accepting a new assignment at the edge of Cardassian space, just so you can quit after you get there? Ben, who are you kidding?"

"Jude—"

"I'm your sister, Ben. I know you. Lie to yourself if you want, but don't lie to me. Or to Dad. If you were serious about resigning, you wouldn't take this assignment. Much less take your son with you. This is about your need to run from your pain. About trying to distance yourself from Jen's death."

Ben slammed his hand on the viewport ledge. "That's enough, Jude."

"But what you don't seem to get yet," Judith had persisted, "is that no matter how far you go, that pain is going to stay with you until you turn around and deal with it."

Ben said nothing. Judith walked back into the living area and began gathering her things. He followed her. "You're leaving?"

"I need to get dirtside. I have to get some sleep before rehearsal tomorrow." She was rummaging through her shoulder bag.

"You could stay here," Ben suggested. "Jake'll be disappointed if you're gone when he wakes up."

Judith refused to look at him. "He'll get over it. Here." Finding the item she sought in her bag, Judith handed her brother a small gift-wrapped package. "I was going to give this to you guys tomorrow, but . . . here, just take it."

Ben accepted the gift. "What is it?"

"Holoprogram," she'd said. "The Early Years of Baseball. A friend of mine designed it. I thought we could all try it next week after I was done in Bradbury City. But maybe it'll give you guys a way to pass the time during the voyage."

"Jude, please don't go yet."

"What do you want from me, Ben? You want me to pretend I don't see what you're doing? Well, I can't. Jen's dead, and that's a tragedy. But you're never going to heal by running from it."

No other words had passed between them as she

walked out, and part of her believed she'd seen her brother and nephew for the last time.

So it was with some surprise that she returned home to Portland a few weeks later to find a subspace message from Starbase Deep Space 9 waiting for her. It was from Ben. Something had obviously happened to him: she could see it in the piercing, purposeful look in his eyes, smiling with an excitement and a self-awareness she hadn't seen in two years. His message was brief and to the point.

"Just thought you'd want to know . . . I've stopped running."

She learned the story later, in subsequent letters and messages from him and Jake, and from their rare visits to Earth: about the discovery of the wormhole and Ben's first contact experience with the entities inside it. And later, his growing connection to the gods and the people of Bajor . . . until he even came to believe that the wormhole beings had brought about his very existence. She'd been skeptical about that last part, and remained so, but she couldn't deny the transformation in him.

Ben had indeed rediscovered himself. But true to her fears, and their father's, she knew also that in doing so, he was lost to his family, maybe forever.

And now Jake, too . . .

Dad stirred, pushing her away. "Go," he whispered, turning back to the window, turning away from her. "Just go. I want to be alone."

Unhappily, Judith respected her father's wishes and withdrew. At the bedroom door she looked back to see him once again as she had found him, hunched over as he stared out the window.

"I just don't know what to do about him, Kasidy," Judith said into the companel late that night, after Joseph had finally fallen asleep. His hopelessness that morning had stayed with her, feeding the stillness and silence of the old house. He simply wasn't the man she once knew. "I knew Ben's disappearance hurt him, but Jake vanishing without a trace so soon after . . . it's like his heart has been torn out. He hasn't been in his kitchen in days. He just sits in his chair by the bedroom window. I think . . . I think he's waiting to die."

Kasidy Yates, her brother's second wife, now more than eight months pregnant, looked back at Judith across the light-years that separated Earth and the planet Bajor and sighed. "It's been hard on everyone. There isn't an hour that passes that I don't think of them both, hoping for word, hoping they'll walk through the door together. But I knew this would be hardest on Joseph. He loves his boys so much. . . ."

Judith smiled. She liked Kasidy. And though they'd only spoken a few times since Ben had announced their marriage last year, she'd warmed up to her new sister-in-law instantly. Maybe part of it was that she was so different from Jennifer. Judith had loved Jake's mother and missed her terribly, but it pleased her that Ben had found a new relationship that hadn't come about merely to fill the void Jen had left in his heart. Kasidy and Ben's love defined itself not by what had been lost, but what they might find together.

"I wish I knew what to tell you, Judith," Kasidy went on. "I call him every week hoping to bolster his spirits, but the conversations have been getting shorter and shorter. I've begun to think that hearing from me is only making his pain worse."

Judith sighed. "He loves you, Kasidy. Don't doubt that."

"I don't," Kasidy assured her. "Not for an instant. I just wish there was some way we could get through to him. Show him that no matter what else, he's about to have a grandchild who's going to need a grandfather. . . ." She trailed off, thoughtful.

"What is it?" Judith asked.

"I just realized . . . maybe there is someone who can get through to him."

The next afternoon, after Dad awoke and resumed his mournful vigil upstairs, Judith waited in the abysmally silent main dining room of the restaurant, wondering what she would do if Kasidy's idea didn't work. His doctor had been clear: Dad needed to get out of that room, and soon. His refusal to take proper care of himself was the reason he'd suffered his collapse in the first place.

A rap on the door. Hushed voices and the unmistakable sound of high-pitched giggles as might come from children. Even muffled by the front door, the sounds seemed to push back the suffocating silence

13

of the house like a cool breeze. Judith went to the door and opened it.

A family stood there: a father, a mother, and two children, a girl and a boy. The father wore a Starfleet uniform. "Ms. Sisko?" he said hopefully.

"Yes?"

"We're the O'Briens. Kasidy Yates asked us to come."

1

All things considered, Dax thought, *this has been one helluva voyage.*

Seated in the center seat of the *U.S.S. Defiant,* Ezri keyed the navigational display on her port command console and reviewed the arc of their journey through the Gamma Quadrant. With more than nine-tenths of the voyage complete, they had made direct first contact with eleven different civilizations, eight of which had expressed interest in follow-up contact by the Federation. In addition, long-range probes had exchanged friendship messages with sixteen other promising contacts. They had recorded or obtained samples of 644 new varieties of life; mapped (with the help of the probes) nearly 1200 cubic light-years of space; witnessed the emergence of a new sentient life-form into this universe; prevented a genocidal civil war; discovered an ineffable artifact with which members of the crew—herself included—had made intimate personal contact; and, somehow, managed to pass *Burning Hearts of Qo'noS* among every member of the crew along the way.

Even Senkowski had finally broken down and read the Klingon romance novel, after a particularly brutal loss in the crew's regular poker game. Once boredom with the usual stakes had set in, Prynn (of course) had suggested betting dares. The game quickly became more popular than ever among the winners, and despised among the losers—Senkowski having been among the latter, after he accepted the dare to read *Burning Hearts of Qo'noS* during a savage hand of five-card stud with Lieutenant Nog.

One helluva voyage indeed.

Of course, they'd also seen their share of tragedies. Ensign Roness had been killed not long into the mission, while under Dax's command; they managed to make enemies of at least three different civilizations (possibly more; transmissions from two of the long-range probes had cut off abruptly, their fate unknown); and many of the crew had been personally affected by some of the things they'd encountered along the way. *Not what we came out here for,* Dax thought, *but we all knew the risks of exploring.* It was, for many, what being in Starfleet was all about. *"Risk,"* she quoted to herself, *"is our business."*

"Did you say something, Lieutenant?"

Dax looked up. Ensign Thirishar ch'Thane had turned from his sciences station to look at her inquiringly. She must have spoken aloud without realizing it.

"Just talking to myself, Ensign," Dax said. She worried about Shar. *Defiant's* science officer had been among those most wounded during their travels, but ironically, not by anything directly attributable to the voyage itself. Shar had been betrothed to three other Andorians back in the Alpha Quadrant, and one of them, Thriss, had grown so despondent by Shar's choice to go on this mission that a month ago she'd committed suicide.

Since receiving that awful news, Shar had been battling his own guilt and despair. Work had been his tonic, but Dax knew that his hours off-duty, when he was most idle, were the hardest for him. Her attempts to engage him as a trained former counselor seemed to help somewhat—he was grateful to talk to someone who understood the emotional and psychological dangers many Andorians faced as a result of their fragile reproductive biology. With Thriss dead, the chances of her surviving bondmates picking up the pieces of their lives to produce the child their culture mandated were slim. Dax feared what would happen to him when they finally returned to Deep Space 9. Would Shar's remaining bondmates embrace him so that together they could work through their shared grief, or would they blame him for what had happened to Thriss, and by extension, to all of them?

All this passed through Dax's mind as Shar looked back at her pleasantly, almost childlike in his demeanor. "Have you studied the data from that biostream yet?" Dax asked.

"Some of it. I regret to report it's looking more and more like a missed opportunity."

Dax nodded ruefully. Three days ago the ship had passed within a light-year of a strange ring of organic molecules, orbiting half an A.U. out from a white dwarf star. Although the readings were anomalous, the captain had elected to launch a probe and press on, rather than investigate directly. Setbacks in their encounters with the Inamuri, the Cheka web weapons, and the so-called "cathedral" had put them behind schedule in returning to the Alpha Quadrant. Add to that the total loss of their replicator systems during the cathedral affair—a development that was now severely limiting their ability to feed themselves and repair damage to the ship—and Vaughn had been compelled to make some tough choices about whether or not to, as he put it, "stop and smell every rose" they came across for the remainder of the voyage.

The cloud ring, however, had been a particularly tempting discovery, especially after the probe had started sending back indications that the organic molecules were far more complex and densely organized than originally thought. Shar believed they'd discovered a new type of spaceborne colonial life. But by then, the unusual star system was well behind them.

"Maybe the next wave of explorers from the Alpha Quadrant will learn more about it," Dax said. That *was* their primary mission objective, after all: to blaze the trail for the ships that would eventually follow. And with ninety percent of their journey done, Dax knew they could all be proud of what they accomplished.

"Yes, sir," Shar replied. "It's just . . . frustrating to come so close to something so new and not being able to study it."

"Remind me to tell you sometime about Jadzia's first attempt to study a Bajoran Orb," Ezri said

Shar tilted his head to one side, intrigued. "I recall reading that report. The Orbs defy conventional analysis, don't they?"

"Yup," Ezri said, then added deliberately, "so far anyway."

In response, Shar's antennae rose up before he turned his attention thoughtfully back to his console.

Dax smiled. Nothing lifted Shar's spirits quite like a new challenge. He was one of those people who became more exhilarated the harder a puzzle was to solve. *Of course,* she thought, *with the Orbs, a good scientist could die from the happiness before he learned anything substantive. I can be so cruel sometimes.*

"Lieutenant, can you come here a moment?"

Dax spun in the command chair to face Bowers, standing at the aft tactical station. *He's got that look—*

She got up and joined him. "What's up, Sam?"

"I was monitoring telemetry from our advance probes," Bowers explained, "when one of them sent back this." *Defiant's* tactical officer nodded toward his console display, indicating a particular waveline in the midst of a chaotic stream of white noise.

Dax blinked, certain she was seeing things. "That

looks almost like—" She looked at him sharply. "Sam, this better not be a joke, or so help me—"

"Ezri, this is no joke," Bowers insisted quietly. "I've triple-checked it, and I'm telling you, it's exactly what it looks like . . . almost."

Dax frowned and stared at the reading. "All right. Give it to me from the top. . . ."

"'Spinach Frittata,'" Dr. Julian Bashir read aloud off the Starfleet ration pack. "'Just add water.'" His face puckering, he replaced the package on the wall rack and grabbed another. "'Ham and Brie on a Quadrotriticale Baguette.'" He put that one back, and picked up a third. "'Denevan Cherries Flambé.'" He arched an eyebrow at that one. It might be worth trying it just to see the flames leap out of the ration pack. But no; he wasn't in the mood for something sweet right now. "Eelshark Salad with Mixed Greens" looked promising, until he read the warning label: "CAUTION: May be toxic to non-Bolians." With a heavy sigh, Bashir finally grabbed a pack labeled "Assorted Grilled Vegetables" and took a seat at a table on the other side of the mess hall. "Have I happened to mentioned that I've come to detest Starfleet field rations?" he asked his dining companions.

"Yes, quite a few times, in fact," Elias Vaughn replied without looking up, seated on the doctor's left and eating from a pack Bashir could see was labeled "Arroz con Pollo." Vaughn consumed a forkful and added, "You're attitude surprises me, Doctor. Colonel Kira once mentioned that you fought to get assigned to DS9 specifically so you could rough it on the frontier."

Bashir winced, recalling that first day on the station. He'd been an overeager junior-grade lieutenant, and as his first official act, he'd successfully managed to offend the station's first officer, then-Major Kira, by describing Bajor and the space around it as a "wilderness" in which he intended to carve out his own legend. Looking back on it, it was a wonder Nerys hadn't decked him.

Bashir looked at Tenmei, seated opposite Vaughn and eagerly devouring her Baba Ghannoush. "Ensign Tenmei's appetite seems unaffected," he noted.

"Learn to live dangerously, Doctor," she suggested playfully. "You'll be *amazed* how much you enjoy everything."

"Remind me to make an appointment for you to see the new counselor when we get back to the station," Bashir said. Tenmei stuck out her tongue at him as he turned back to Vaughn. "I don't suppose Nog has had any luck at all with the replicators?" he asked.

Vaughn shook his head. "Shall I remind you *why* we're eating field rations in the first place?"

Bashir gave up. "Touché, Commander." Being reminded that the replicator systems had been sacrificed in order to save his life, as well as those of Ezri and Nog, was an effective way to silence his complaints. Until the *Defiant* returned to Deep Space 9, meals would be restricted to the ration packs, and whatever they could cook from the limited raw ingredients stored in the cargo bays.

"You know," Vaughn said at length, "back in '04, I was in a situation much worse than this one."

Tenmei leaned over in Bashir's direction. "Run for it, Doctor, before he gains a head of steam," she advised.

"I remember it well," Vaughn said, seemingly oblivious to Tenmei's warning. "I was assigned to a ship that had been forced to go quiet for a month on the wrong side of the Tholian border. No replicators, no holodecks, complete radio silence. Just eighty-five people with nothing but ration packs, a library computer, and a lot of imagination."

"I told you," Tenmei said to Bashir in a singsong voice.

"You know, sir," Bashir got out, "that sounds fascinating, but I just realized that I left something on in the medical bay—"

Vaughn's hand closed around Bashir's wrist, refusing to let him leave. "I can still recall Crewman Richards stealing the rats from the biolab for meatloaf—"

"He did *not*," Tenmei said.

Vaughn arched an eyebrow at his daughter. "Who's telling this story, Ensign? Anyway, the point is," Vaughn said, releasing Bashir and grabbing the tall drink at the commander's elbow, "that compared to many who came before us, we live and work in luxury, even when deprived of some of the things we take for granted."

"Point taken," Bashir assured him.

Vaughn drained the last of his iced tea and smiled.

"That was delicious. And you haven't even started your meal yet."

Bashir looked at his unopened ration pack and smiled sheepishly. "I think I'll save it for later," he said as he rose from the table. "For when I'm *really* hungry." Pack in hand, Bashir nodded to his fellow officers and started for the door.

Tenmei laughed. Vaughn smiled and shook his head.

As Bashir was crossing the room, the mess hall doors parted and Ezri walked in, carrying a padd. *Uh-oh,* Bashir thought. *I know that expression. Something's up. . . .*

"Hi," he said as they met up with each other. "You okay?"

"What? Oh, yeah. Just a report I need to make to the commander. Enjoy your dinner?"

Bashir held up his ration pack. "Decided to save it. See you when you get off duty?"

"Sure. I'll even grab one myself and we can eat together."

"It's a date," Bashir said. "Try not to work too hard."

Ezri laughed. "Where the hell were you when I decided to transfer to command?"

Bashir was already in the corridor. "Being supportive," he called as the doors closed behind him.

Dax walked toward the table, trying not to rush. Judging from the look on Julian's face, he'd figured out immediately that she had something to tell Vaughn. She hoped she wasn't that obvious. Then again, Julian's enhanced perceptions helped him to pick up on visual cues that might escape other people. Especially in someone as close to him as Ezri.

"Commander, Ensign," Dax began. "Hope I'm not interrupting."

"Actually, I was just about to get going," Prynn said, rising from her chair. "I promised Mikaela I'd look over her ideas for improving the navigational deflector."

"If you have time, stop by my cabin later," Vaughn said. "I found a Rowatu recording in the ship's database that I don't think you've heard."

Prynn smiled. "Okay. 2100?"

Vaughn nodded.

Prynn bid Dax goodbye and departed the mess hall.

"It's nice to see you two getting along so well, now," Dax told Vaughn. "If you don't mind my saying so, I think it agrees with both of you."

Vaughn sighed, staring after his daughter. "Lot of wasted years to make up for. We've learned quite a bit about each other on this voyage."

"She's a good officer, too," Dax added. "Quick, dedicated, talented. You should be proud. The next generation of Vaughns is off to a good start."

Vaughn snorted. "Fortunately for her, she's a Tenmei through and through." He turned to meet Dax's gaze, then glanced toward the padd she was holding. "So what's up?"

"I was hoping you could tell me," Dax said as she took the seat Prynn had vacated. "Sam was reviewing the datastream from the last pair of probes we sent out when one of them detected an anomaly in one of the narrower subspace strata, a layer nobody we know uses for communications because of the high background interference. There was so much white noise, in fact, Bowers admits he almost missed it. He passed it through the filters a few times to be sure, and there's no longer any doubt: it's a Starfleet transponder signal." Dax handed Vaughn the padd for his perusal. "One of our people is out here, where nobody else from the Federation has ever been, as far as we know. But the signal's not like any that Bowers or I have ever seen before. The beam is much stronger, as if it was designed to punch through all the subspace interference it was being sent through. But since ordinarily we wouldn't look for a communications signal in that stratum, it made me wonder if it might be connected to Starfleet Intelligence or . . ." Dax paused, stopped by the look on Vaughn's face. "Are you all right?"

Vaughn was frowning. Not in confusion or contemplation, as if he'd found some new puzzle to solve, but in what Dax could only characterize as denial. The look crossed his face for only a second before returning to the neutral expression he usually wore.

"Who else knows about this?" Vaughn asked quietly, still studying the data.

"Just Sam," Dax said. "Is there something—"

"Make sure it stays that way," Vaughn interrupted. "I don't want either of you sharing this with anyone. Return to the bridge and engage the cloaking device immediately. Then alter course to trace this signal back to the source, maximum warp. If the crew asks—tell them not to." Vaughn stood up and started to leave, taking the padd with him.

"You want to tell me—"

"No," Vaughn snapped. "Just carry out my orders, Lieutenant." At the mess hall door Vaughn stopped. "One other thing: The *Sagan*'s taken a beating the last couple of months. I want her better than ready in case we need her. Have a complete battery of systems diagnostics run from bow to stern, and an overhaul on the navigational array. Put Tenmei on it."

Dax frowned. "All right," she assented, "but it'll take time."

"Whatever it takes," was Vaughn's response. "Just do it." He stepped across the threshold and the door closed behind him.

Dax watched the commander go, wondering what new crisis had just been sparked.

When Vaughn reached his quarters, he found he couldn't recall how he'd gotten there. He knew he must have traversed the corridor from the mess hall, ridden the turbolift up to deck one, and passed through the door of his cabin, but he had no memory of making the journey. Only one thing occupied his thoughts, one impossible thing.

Setting the padd down, he touched a contact on the back wall of his cabin, causing the basin to emerge. He held his hands under the faucet and cool water gathered into his cupped hands. Bending over, he brought the water to his face, splashing his eyes, soaking his beard. He repeated the process, again and again, realizing that each breath was becoming more difficult. He stopped and stared at his hands. They were shaking.

Steady, Elias. You'll hyperventilate or worse, push that hundred-year-old heart of yours right over the cliff.

Vaughn closed his eyes and steadied his breathing and heart rate, using a Vulcan meditation technique he'd learned . . . when? Forty? Fifty years ago? So hard to keep the events of his life straight in his mind sometimes. When he opened his eyes again, his aged reflection stared back at him from the mirror above the basin. Water dripped from his silver hair, forming rivulets in the deep lines of his face. Dark hollows surrounded his eyes. *So many damn years . . .*

Vaughn grabbed a towel and patted himself dry. Then he picked up the padd and collapsed on his bunk.

There was no mistaking the transponder signal. He'd committed the code to memory decades ago. But why here, and why now, of all times? He sifted through the possibilities, and decided the only answer he could believe was the one that made no sense at all.

But if it was true . . . if the trail they were now following led to the *Valkyrie,* then the closure he'd long sought for the disastrous mission to Uridi'si might finally be within his reach.

He fell asleep with the padd clutched to his chest, dreaming of the dead.

2

The world as she knew it had ended.

"Place both your hands on the tome and speak as I do: I, Asarem Wadeen . . ."

Her shaking hands rested on the book. Flecks of another's blood stained her smooth brown skin. She thought she heard herself say the words as the magistrate bade her, but her voice seemed too distant, as if she were very far away from what was happening.

Bajoran security had thrown her to the floor of the Promenade's meeting hall in the first few seconds, attempting to protect her from further weapons fire and from the chaos that had erupted. Screams filled the room, mingling with the sound of the transporter beam that had allowed the assassin to escape. People pushed against each other, some attempting to flee in panic, others trying to regain control of the situation. She'd heard Lieutenant Ro shouting orders—

". . . to uphold the laws of Bajor and to act honorably as custodian of the Bajoran people . . ."

—General Lenaris, searching the room with his eyes for accomplices; Admiral Akaar, speaking urgently into his combadge; Colonel Kira, rushing toward the body, demanding an emergency transport to the infirmary; blood everywhere—

". . . that I will protect and defend the Bajoran people from all foes, within and without . . ."

A half-dozen security people had taken her from the scene, three in front of her, one on either side of her holding tightly to her upper arms as they ushered her swiftly through the dim Cardassian corridors of the space station. A sixth deputy was at her back, one hand clamped to her shoulder, pushing her forward—

". . . that I will face the future fearlessly . . ."

Phasers drawn and held high all around her, a small irrational part of Asarem had wondered briefly if she was being taken to her execution. Only later, after they'd sequestered her in her VIP quarters, when Supreme Magistrate Hegel arrived with Deep Space 9's Bajoran doctor and confirmed the assassination, had she realized fully that she was not about to die, but that her life would never again be the same. From that day forward it belonged to Bajor, and Bajor alone.

". . . and that I will conduct myself with truth and

honor, and with faith in the guidance of the Prophets . . ."

Shakaar was dead.

". . . pledging my life and my *pagh* to the service of Bajor."

She felt the tome slip away as the magistrate closed the book and bowed her head. "Walk with the Prophets, First Minister Asarem."

Too late, Ro Laren saw the truth. Hiziki Gard, aide to the Trill ambassador and security liaison for the Federation delegations, had played her from the beginning. For weeks he'd lived and worked aboard the station unobtrusively. He had consistently deferred to Ro's authority as chief of security, seemingly content to work within, rather than attempt to override, her security precautions. He had flattered her and approached her socially as kindred spirits. He'd even flirted with her. He had done it all . . . just so he'd know exactly how to undermine her security measures in order to kill Shakaar.

Several of her deputies swarmed the room, some taking statements from witnesses or holding them for further questioning, others ushering delegates out of the meeting hall, away from the crime scene. She saw Councillor zh'Thane and Admiral Akaar in deep, frantic conversation with a dismayed Seljin Gandres, the Trill ambassador. The Cardassians—Gul Macet and Cleric Ekosha—had gathered in one corner of the room around a pale and shaken Vedek Yevir, who looked as if he was trying very hard not to vomit. Some of the other guests were jabbering hysterically, none louder than Quark, who was protesting Corporal Hava's attempts to usher him out. "Laren! Laren, please!"

"Not now," she growled. Sergeant Shul passed close to her, and Ro seized his arm. "Get the rest of these people out of here. I want the room sealed, and I want to start interviewing witnesses immediately, starting with the Trills. Have you heard from Etana yet?"

"She checked in a minute ago," the older, gray-haired deputy said. "Minister Asarem is secure in her quarters."

"The hell she is," Ro said. "Keep the habitat ring locked down but evacuate the sector with Asarem's quarters, sections 060 through 120, every level, I don't care who's living there. I want guards inside and outside her quarters at all times, surveillance in every corridor, patrols on the crossover bridges, and situation reports every thirty minutes. Move."

Suddenly Taran'atar was next to her, his faced knotted in concern, his words brief and to the point: "The assassin may still be aboard the station."

Ro took his meaning: he was volunteering to go hunt for the killer—as only a Jem'Hadar could. "Go," Ro said.

Taran'atar nodded once and shrouded, becoming invisible, and for a disconcerting moment she felt grateful to the Founders for engineering their soldiers so well.

"Ro."

Ro turned, finding herself under the glare of Fleet Admiral Leonard James Akaar. Nearby, Councillor

31

zh'Thane and Ambassador Gandres looked on. Though they all appeared concerned, the Trill ambassador seemed the most visibly upset by far. "Yes, Admiral?"

"How did this happen?" Akaar demanded. "You were supposed to have—"

"I was supposed to have been securing this ceremony from outside forces that might have reasons to disrupt it," Ro interrupted hotly. "Not from one of the Federation's own security representatives!"

Akaar's eyes narrowed. "Maybe if your own precautions had been more effective, Gard would not have been able to circumvent them." Ever since her court martial over the Garon II debacle, Akaar had never attempted to hide his disapproval of Ro. If he'd had his way, she'd probably be in the Federation penal facility right now instead of serving as Deep Space 9's chief of security.

"And maybe if the Federation's screening procedures were more effective, he would never have been part of the delegation to begin with," Ro countered quietly. "You want to blame me for this disaster, Admiral? Fine. But then maybe you should ask why a member of the Trill ambassadorial staff would want to kill the first minister just as Shakaar was about to thumb the agreement to make Bajor part of the Federation."

"Precisely the question I want to ask, Lieutenant," a voice at her shoulder said. General Lenaris Holem of the Bajoran Militia matched Akaar's stern gaze before turning it on zh'Thane and Gandres. "Can you explain this, Admiral? Councillor? Ambassador?"

The delegates looked at one another but said nothing, Ambassador Gandres becoming paler by the second.

It didn't take long for Dr. Girani to make her pronouncement: Shakaar had died instantly, and the brutal damage done to his brain stem and medulla oblongata ruled out any hope of resuscitation. With emotion cracking her voice, Girani called the time of death at 1119.

The bladed projectile that had slammed into Shakaar's neck had been absurdly redundant. As if the impact damage alone hadn't been enough, the tip contained a phaser charge that activated on contact with Shakaar's uppermost vertebrae, disintegrating the back of the first minister's lower skull. Kira had never heard of a more vicious weapon.

She had stood by throughout the ordeal, feeling helpless. In a matter of seconds a single act had unraveled everything. The assassin had killed not only Shakaar, but quite possibly Bajor's future with the Federation. Everything else the day had brought—Yevir's startling breakthrough in forging a relationship with the Cardassians that went beyond politics, the long-awaited return of the lost Tears of the Prophets—was now tainted by what had followed. The murder of the first minister at the hands of a Federation national and a member of a diplomatic delegation would be the undoing of everything they all had worked for during the last seven years.

Magistrate Hegel, who had arrived in the Infirmary in time to witness Girani's confirmation of the death, departed immediately, no doubt to deal with the succession. There could be no delay in the transfer of power to Asarem. Now more than ever, Bajor needed a leader.

Girani had left with the magistrate, giving Kira a few minutes alone with the body before the doctor returned to begin her autopsy. Perhaps Girani knew that Kira would need those minutes . . . would need the closure of saying goodbye and the reality of Shakaar's lifeless, murdered body to prepare herself for what lay ahead.

It was difficult for her to look at Edon's blank face, the bloody absorbant pad that had been draped around his neck, the still chest that no longer rose and fell. Unbidden, she remembered those rare mornings after they'd shared a night of passion, when she'd awoken to find him still asleep beside her. She'd watch the rise and fall of his chest, stroke his skin, feel his life beneath her fingers.

So much had changed over the years. Once they'd been friends fighting side by side in the resistance, then lovers swept together by their mutual desire to bring stability to post-Occupation Bajor. Eventually, Kira and Shakaar had drifted apart, as lovers sometimes do. Their romance had ended amicably more than two years ago, but during the last few months, something had changed.

The Attainder that had separated her from the Bajoran spiritual community notwithstanding, she and Edon had become estranged in a way that had puzzled and hurt her at first, then even made her question her ability to trust him as the leader of Bajor. Now she would never know why. Nor would she ever learn what had made him so manipulative in recent weeks, or why he'd become vindictive toward the Cardassians after working so hard at first to help them in the aftermath of the Dominion War.

Was that why he was killed? she wondered. Had Gard, or someone close to him, also noticed Shakaar's inexplicable behavior and been so confounded by it that they'd felt compelled to kill him? As far as she was aware, only she and Asarem had known of his duplicity with the Cardassians, and unless Kira was willing to entertain the notion that Asarem had conspired to kill Shakaar in order to seize power—

Steady, Nerys. That kind of speculation before the facts are in could be as damaging as the assassination itself.

But what if someone in the Cardassian delegation had found out about Shakaar's orders to have Asarem scuttle the Bajoran–Cardassian talks? One of them might have wanted revenge. But to use Gard? What could the connection be?

Or were there elements in the Federation, or Trill specifically, who wanted to sabotage Bajor's admittance?

Every possibility contained its own unique component of horror, because each one meant that there were forces at large willing to harm Bajor. And that was something Kira Nerys would not allow again. Whoever was behind this, for whatever reason, Kira would learn the truth and expose it, no matter where it led. That was the vow she made as she stood over Shakaar's body.

She stroked his cold cheek with the back of her hand. *Never again,* she swore. Then she squared her shoulders and marched out of the surgical bay.

Never.

3

Her back resting against the antigrav dolly, Prynn Tenmei reached up with both hands through the access panel beneath the belly of the shuttlecraft *Sagan*. She was up to her elbows in isolinear circuitry and subspace field coils, prying loose a stubborn ODN cable that she discovered was nearing the end of its operational life, when she lost her grip on the hyperspanner in her hand, catching it full in the face.

"Dammit dammit dammit . . ." Hearing her expletives echoing through the otherwise empty shuttlebay, Prynn kicked the flight deck with her heel, sliding the dolly out from under the shuttle so she could sit up to rub her bruised cheek. Bad enough she'd been exiled to the shuttlebay to work on a craft that was hardly in need of more maintenance, she didn't appreciate adding injury to insult.

"Maybe you should have asked the bridge to lower the gravity in here before you tried that," a voice said behind her. "Fewer accidents. Well, less painful ones, anyway."

Prynn looked over her shoulder and scowled, waving the spanner. "Yeah, but if I throw this at you in one-gee, it'll hurt more," she cautioned. "Sir."

Lieutenant Nog, standing near the port shuttlebay entrance with his hands behind his back, grinned back. "Nice save, Ensign. And just to show you there are no hard feelings . . ." Nog brought both his hands out, holding two tall glasses of something frothy and white. A clear straw stuck out buoyantly from each one.

"Oh, those look good," Prynn said.

Nog walked over to her and handed Prynn one of the glasses before sitting on the deck next to her. "Ensign Lankford mentioned you'd been in here since 0800 without taking a break. I figured you were on a roll and wouldn't want to hit the mess hall—I know what that's like—but I thought you'd spare time for a milk shake."

Prynn accepted the shake gratefully and toasted Nog with it. "May the Blessed Exchequer deliver you from Destitution, Lieutenant."

"I'll drink to that," Nog said, clinking her glass.

Prynn wrapped her lips around the straw, then stopped, looking at Nog suspiciously. "Tell me you didn't puree any tube grubs for this."

"No way. I learned my lesson the first time." A few months back, at Nog's urging, Prynn had sampled a tube grub for the first time. She'd spat it out like a projectile, right past Nog's ear. "Mine's a grub

38

shake," he explained. "Yours is milk and ice cream. Lieutenant Candlewood mixed them himself."

She eyed the glasses skeptically. "They look the same."

"Trust me, Prynn, I wouldn't do that to you. Cheers."

Prynn took a slurp and closed her eyes, rapture filling her face. "God, that's good. Thanks, Nog. I'm sorry I doubted you."

Nog grinned. "My pleasure. Glad it helped." He took a sip from his own straw and almost immediately spat it out in disgust, spraying the hull of the *Sagan*.

"Hey, watch it!" Prynn cried, startled. "What's the matter?"

Nog was still trying to spit the remaining droplets. "Milk and ice cream!" he said, grimacing.

"Both of them? Hmm, that's ironic." Prynn resumed slurping her shake. "Lieutenant Candlewood strikes again."

Nog regarded his glass disgustedly. "I'm gonna get even with that guy, so help me. . . ." Candlewood had recently taken on the role of the ship's resident practical joker, and this marked the third time Nog had fallen victim to one of his pranks.

"Maybe he has a crush on you and this is just his way of expressing it," Prynn said pleasantly.

"Oh, thanks," Nog said sarcastically. "As if I wasn't sick enough from the milk shake."

Prynn chuckled. "How's Shar doing?"

"Better, I think," Nog said, then shrugged. "Hard to be sure, sometimes. But I think he's passed the worst of it. At least, until we get back to the Alpha Quadrant."

Prynn nodded. Although it wasn't discussed openly, word had circulated among the crew about the news Shar had received last month—the worst possible on a voyage like this one: the death of a loved one back home. Dad had given Prynn a general idea of the circumstances, and her heart went out to Shar. Having endured her own share of loss, she understood what Shar must be going through.

Nog set down his unfinished shake. "Hey, hand that over," Prynn told him, finishing the last of the ice cream in her own glass. "No point in letting it go to waste."

Nog shook his head and passed his shake over to Prynn. "So what did you do to get banished down here, anyway?"

Prynn rolled her eyes. "I wish I knew. I haven't been on the bridge in three days, ever since the course change."

Nog nodded. "Have you talked to your father—I mean, Commander Vaughn?"

"Is that why you came down here?" Prynn asked. "To see if my relationship to Vaughn made me privy to what was going on topside?"

Nog shrugged innocently. "Not at all!" At Prynn's dubious look he admitted, "Well, not entirely."

"Nog . . ."

"It was Senkowski's idea!" No protested. "He thought someone should ask you, since even Dax and Bowers have been tight-lipped about the whole thing."

"Let me guess, you drew the short straw?"

"Uh . . . did you like the milk shakes?" Nog asked hopefully.

Prynn sighed. "One thing you should know about my father, Nog, as present circumstance should aptly prove," she said, gesturing at the shuttlebay around them, "is that no one has ever accused him of nepotism. And with good reason. Whatever's going on, he hasn't told me. I've hardly talked to him the last few days. And I'm usually the last person to find out anything around here."

"I'm sorry, Prynn," Nog said. "You'd think the only son of the Grand Nagus would know better than to try to take advantage of your relationship to the commander. I know how irritating that can be. Uncle Quark's waiters have been falling over themselves to engage me in conversation ever since my father took over the Ferengi Alliance."

"Hey, it's all right," Prynn assured him. "No hard feelings, honest. I suppose it's only natural that people assume I'm somehow more inside the loop than anyone else where my father's concerned. I wish it were true, but . . ." She shrugged. "The milk shakes *were* great, by the way."

"I'm glad," Nog said. "It's funny . . . I never really thought about it much, but you, me, Shar, Jake . . . we're all the children of some pretty important people who have intersected at DS9."

"I dunno about that," Prynn said. "My father's not a world leader, or a Federation councillor, or a religious-icon-slash-Starfleet-captain. Vaughn isn't quite that prominent."

"You know, that reminds me of something else I've been meaning to ask . . ."

41

Prynn sighed. "Go ahead."

"Well, it's just that . . . he's been in Starfleet for eighty years, right? Why is he still just a commander?"

Prynn laughed. "You're wondering if he somehow managed to piss off the wrong people at some point in his career?"

"Well . . . yeah, I guess," Nog admitted.

"Wouldn't surprise me if he did," Prynn said wryly. "But that's not the reason."

"Then why—?"

"Nog, how big do you think the Tal Shiar's file is on, say, Jean-Luc Picard?"

"Pretty big, I'd think."

"And how big a file do you think they have on Elias Vaughn?"

Nog shrugged. "I have no idea."

"Then I'll tell you—they probably *don't* have one on him. At least, I'd bet they didn't before he was re-assigned to DS9. By advancing no higher than commander, and taking no long-term assignments for the last eighty years, he's managed to go relatively unnoticed. Anonymity was a powerful tool on the kinds of missions he used to go on. It's how he survived."

"But he's given it up," Nog said. Becoming first officer of Deep Space 9 and commander officer of the *Defiant* had to be like stepping into a spotlight for somebody like Vaughn.

Prynn shrugged. "Times change. People change. I don't completely understand the circumstances that led him to take his current assignment—all that Orb business is lost on me, frankly—but I do know how bitter he'd become about his life during the last ten years. Whatever happened to convince him to make the changes he's made, it's renewed him. I think he felt trading his anonymity for a new lease on life was worth it."

Nog seemed to consider what Prynn told him. Then he said, "Candlewood has a theory about what the course change is all about."

"Oh?"

"He thinks it's Cardassians."

Prynn frowned. "What leads him to suspect that?"

"You know he periodically checks the logs of computer use on board?"

Prynn nodded. That was no secret. Standard operating procedure for a ship's computer techs.

"Well, he noticed that there'd been a download of a classified file on the planet Uridi'si three days ago. That's nearest to Cardassian space. And Commander Vaughn is the only person on board with clearance high enough to download the entire file."

Prynn was silent a moment, slurping the last of her second milk shake. "That doesn't really prove anything."

"I suppose not," Nog said. "Still—"

"Vaughn to Nog."

Nog reached for his combadge and tapped it. "Go ahead."

"Report to my ready room immediately, Lieutenant."

"Aye, sir. I'm on my way." Nog tapped off and turned to Prynn. "Looks like something's up."

Prynn smiled. "Told you, Nog: I'm the last person to find out anything around here."

The look on Nog's face when he walked into the captain's ready room was priceless, Sam thought. The kid was so eager to be in the loop he actually looked like he was fighting to keep a smile off his face. *That's all about to change.*

Vaughn sat behind his desk. Sam and Dax stood off to one side in the cramped cabin, leaving the single guest chair for the chief engineer. "Thanks for coming, Nog. Have a seat," Vaughn told him.

Nog sat down and waited while the commander consulted something on his desktop display before he finally looked at the young officer. "I want to be clear about something from the onset, Lieutenant," Vaughn began. "Nothing discussed during this meeting leaves this room."

Nog nodded. "I understand, sir."

"Dax. Tell him."

Nog turned to *Defiant*'s X.O. as she launched into an explanation of Sam's discovery of the Starfleet transponder signal. "We've traced it to a class-M planet that the *Defiant* is presently orbiting. Attempts to scan the surface in order to pinpoint the source of the transmission have instead turned up something else: the wreckage of a Jem'Hadar attack ship."

Dax let the revelation sink in, pausing to give Nog a chance to ask questions. Sam had a pretty good idea what he must be thinking: *The Dominion was parsecs distant, and* Defiant'*s course had been plotted delib-*

erately to keep it as far from the Founders' borders as possible. So what was a Jem'Hadar ship doing out here? They were the same thoughts that still ran through Sam's mind.

"Any indication what destroyed it?" Nog asked.

"No," Dax said. "No sign of survivors, either, although the evidence is far from conclusive. Heavy atmospheric disturbances are making sensor readings unreliable beyond a certain point. The only way we're going to learn more is to go down there,"

"I'll be leading the away team," Vaughn said to Nog. "You and Lieutenant Bowers will be going with me to assess the wreckage and determine what caused the crash. And to pinpoint the transponder signal. We beam down in thirty minutes."

"Yes, sir," Nog said and, believing the meeting adjourned, stood up to leave.

"Nog," Vaughn said, stopping him. "I'm sure I don't have to remind you that the discovery of a Starfleet transponder signal at the site of a destroyed Dominion ship in the Gamma Quadrant is a sensitive matter requiring the utmost discretion. Nevertheless, I'm repeating my initial instruction: this isn't to be discussed with anyone outside this room."

"I understand, sir," Nog said. *No trace of a smile,* Sam noted. *He knows we're in deep. And just like the rest of us, the number one question on his mind is "How much deeper will it get?"*

4

"What do you mean, he killed First Minister Shakaar?"

"I mean exactly that, Madam President," Charivretha zh'Thane said, and with exacting detail, described to Trill leader Elekzia Maz, whose shocked faced stared back at her from the wardroom viewscreen, the murder zh'Thane herself had witnessed by Hiziki Gard.

"This is impossible," Maz insisted.

"I saw it with own eyes, Madam President."

"Where is Ambassador Gandres? I want to speak with him."

"He's being questioned by Deep Space 9's chief of security," zh'Thane said. "He may be a while."

"The Bajorans can't possibly believe this despicable act was sanctioned by the Trill government."

"They don't know what to believe, Madam President," zh'Thane told her honestly. "And under the circumstances, questioning the other members of the Trill delegation is a logical first step. For what it's worth, Gandres is conducting himself admirably. As a gesture of sincerity, he has chosen not to invoke diplomatic immunity. But it might also help if Trill were to issue a statement condemning the murder, and to make a pledge of cooperation such as Bajor may require."

"Yes, of course," Maz agreed. "We'll cooperate fully."

"It would also be a show of good faith to send Deep Space 9 whatever data you have on this Hiziki Gard."

Maz nodded. "I'll convene my cabinet to discuss the situation immediately. You have my word, Councillor, an official statement will be released within the day. I personally will contact the new first minister to make a formal declaration of regret and apology, and to offer any assistance Bajor may need in this time of crisis."

"Thank you, Madam President."

Maz shook her head. "In five lifetimes I've never faced anything like this."

"It is a difficult time for all of us," zh'Thane acknowledged.

"Does the Federation Council—?"

"They are aware of the situation," zh'Thane said gravely. "I am acting on their behalf to try to keep the political situation from deteriorating further."

"I don't envy you the task ahead," Maz said. "Good luck to you, Councillor."

"To all of us, Madam President."

Maz closed the link, and as the wardroom screen reverted to the Great Seal of the Federation, zh'Thane slowly moved to the meeting table and fell heavily into the nearest chair. She covered her eyes with one hand and fought back tears, wishing more than ever that Shar was with her now.

In the observation room Akaar stood leaning into the viewscreen and frowned as he watched Ro Laren question Ambassador Gandres inside the security office's interrogation chamber. Ro sat opposite Gandres at a bare metal table in the middle of the chamber, surrounded by dismal gray walls and deliberately oppressive illumination. Throughout the first hour the ambassador had continued to insist he had no foreknowledge of Gard's intentions toward Shakaar, claiming that his aide had been assigned to him from the Trill Diplomatic Corps before they left for Deep Space 9. Part of Gard's assignment had been to work with station personnel to ensure the security of the Federation dignitaries. Beyond that, Gandres apparently knew Gard only as an easygoing but consummate professional—in a way that seemed to come so easily to the joined, Gandres had added with a hint of bitterness.

Ro persisted with questions about the assassin: behavior he'd exhibited, conversations he and Gandres had had, habits the ambassador had observed, other people Gard had contact with while he was aboard the station.

Gandres had been able to offer little insight . . .

save that he'd seen Gard and Ro socializing at the Ferengi bar on the Promenade recently.

Akaar's frown deepened.

The admiral turned as the door into the small, dark observation room opened, admitting General Lenaris, who had spent the last hour meeting with Minister Asarem, and in contact with the leaders of the Militia on Bajor.

"How bad is it?" Akaar asked.

"Bad," Lenaris confirmed. "We've managed to implement an information blackout until the first minister can address the Bajoran people, but once this gets out, global shock will set in, the accusations will start, and the isolationists will have a field day."

"How is the first minister?"

"As she should be, Admiral," Lenaris said. "Concerned for her people, and determined to take whatever steps are necessary to ensure their safety from outside threats."

"None of us wanted this, General," Akaar said.

"I don't doubt that," Lenaris replied. "But it's happened. And if some Bajorans had doubts before about unity with the Federation, then more will very soon."

"And where do you stand on the question?"

Lenaris met his gaze. "I'm a soldier, Admiral. I stand with the people I took an oath to protect. Always."

"But do you not see? This is what the assassin wanted: to divide us. We must work together to right this situation, General, or Bajor and the Federation will both lose."

"That may be," Lenaris conceded. "But only the first minister can make that decision, and I suspect she will very soon. We're to meet her in the wardroom in twenty-five minutes, together with Councillor zh'Thane, Colonel Kira, and Lieutenant Ro."

As if on cue, the door opened again and Ro walked in. A glance at the viewscreen showed Gandres was no longer in the interrogation room.

"He claims to know nothing substantive about Gard or the assassination," Ro said immediately, "other than what we all saw in the meeting hall. I believe him. But that doesn't necessarily mean that this is the rogue action he seems to think it is."

"What do you mean?" Lenaris asked.

"Gard might have acted alone, for reasons of his own," Ro conceded. "But a couple of things the ambassador said make me think there's more to it. First and foremost, Gandres didn't select him to be on his staff. According to the ambassador, Gard was assigned to him from the Trill Diplomatic Corps out of the blue, specifically for the Bajor assignment."

"That proves nothing, Lieutenant," Akaar said.

"Not by itself, no," Ro admitted. "But, Admiral . . . Gard was a joined Trill. That was something I hadn't really considered until Gandres reminded me. During my own association with Gard, he implied he'd had many past lives."

"I do not see—"

"Admiral, have you ever heard of a joined Trill committing any violent crime? Much less a cold, calculated murder? I confess I'm not entirely familiar with how it works, but my understanding is that the screening process they employ is designed to match hosts and symbionts in such a way that joined Trills are invariably stable personalities. I know from Lieutenant Dax that anomalies do occur from time to time, but unless Gard is one of those rare mismatched Trills, then the murder of First Minister Shakaar couldn't have been simply the rogue action of a madman. It had to have a purpose." Akaar seemed to ponder that for a moment, and then Ro added, "This is still all guesswork, though. To be certain, I need access to Gard's official and personal files from Trill."

"Councillor zh'Thane is seeing to that," Akaar said, then switched tacks. "Have the station's sensors revealed anything about the transporter beam Gard used to escape?"

Ro shook her head. "My people are still working on it, but Gard somehow managed to scramble the sensors just before he beamed out."

Akaar muttered a Capellan curse. "I've apprised Captain Mello of the situation. The *Gryphon* is conducting its own sensor sweep of the Bajoran system even as we speak." The admiral looked at Lenaris. "We should locate Colonel Kira and join Councillor zh'Thane to await the first minister."

Lenaris nodded and the two men started out. Ro said, "Wait, where are you going?"

The general looked at her grimly. "To face the music, Lieutenant. And you're invited, too."

* * *

First Minister Asarem entered the wardroom under guard. To Kira's eye, she looked considerably better than she had when she'd been evacuated from the meeting hall. Everyone rose to their feet as she entered, their eyes following her as she immediately took her place at the head of the meeting table. Kira and the other attendees sat down only when Asarem did, and maintained a respectful silence until the first minister spoke.

Asarem surveyed the table, meeting the eyes of each person with an impenetrable and unflinching calm. *Good,* Kira thought as the minister's eyes fell on her. *Make sure no one has any doubt who's in charge here. Every Bajoran will look to you for strength now. And everyone else will judge Bajor by the kind of leader you are.*

"In forty minutes," Asarem began, "I am boarding the *Li Nalas* and departing Deep Space 9 for Bajor to address an emergency session of the Chamber of Ministers. I will thereafter address the Bajoran people."

"What will you say, First Minister?" Kira asked.

Asarem looked directly at Councillor zh'Thane and Admiral Akaar when she answered. "I'll tell them the truth. That after the assassination of First Minister Shakaar by a member of the Federation diplomatic delegation, Bajor cannot, in good conscience, accept the Federation's invitation to become a member at this time. I will order a full investigation into the murder of Shakaar, and I will ask the chamber to pass a resolution to reevaluate the need for Starfleet's continued presence on Deep Space 9."

Silence descended on the wardroom. Even Kira was stunned. "First Minister, please," zh'Thane began, "don't do this."

"What would you have me do instead, Ambassador?" Asarem asked pragmatically. "Is it really the position of the Federation Council that Bajor can still move forward with the Federation now? That the Bajoran people will accept the heinous assassination of its lawfully elected leader as a trivial inconvenience? Is that *your* position, Councillor?"

"My position," zh'Thane answered, "is that the Federation is not Bajor's enemy, First Minister. We are its friends. It is a friendship both parties have cultivated for over seven years. A friendship that during that time has endured one crisis after another, one threat after another, and always emerged stronger. It is a friendship that has never, and *must* never, falter in the darkest times, when friendships are most sorely tested. And as a friend, I pledge to you that the Federation will not falter in its commitment to Bajor now. We share the grief of the Bajoran people. We are saddened and outraged by the assassination of First Minister Shakaar. But we must not allow this act of evil to poison our resolve to join together. Shakaar was murdered in the act of committing to that union. Will you now render his last great labor—and the labors of Captain Sisko—meaningless?"

For a moment Asarem's eyes sought out Kira's. No doubt she, like Nerys, wondered how Shakaar's "last great labor" and the secret manner in which he had pursued it, played into his death. But whether Shakaar had been duplicitous or not, Kira had come to believe Asarem had too much integrity to malign his memory, however justified it might be. And the councillor wasn't stupid: she had to know what evoking the name of the Emissary would mean in this context, and counted on it.

But Asarem clearly wasn't going to be swayed that easily. "And how precisely will the Federation demonstrate its commitment, Councillor? What will it do?"

It was Akaar who answered. "What we have always done. Remain true to Bajor. We will support and cooperate fully with your investigation, First Minister. Like you, we also want the truth."

"And yet, the truth has so far proven elusive, hasn't it, Admiral? The assassin, himself a Federation representative sent here by his government, has escaped."

"Maybe not," Ro said.

All eyes looked at her. "Ro?" Kira said.

"Forgive me, Colonel, but the more I think about the circumstances surrounding the murder, the less certain I am that everything transpired as most of us seem to be assuming."

"Are you about to suggest that First Minister Shakaar isn't truly dead, Lieutenant?" Asarem asked, almost with a tinge of amusement.

"First Minister, no. That isn't what I mean. What I mean is that there are limits to what his killer could have accomplished on his own. And so far, there's no evidence to suggest Gard acted with accomplices here on the station."

"Meaning what?" Lenaris asked.

"Meaning that when he beamed away, where could he have gone?"

"Our assumption has been that he had a cloaked ship standing by in order to escape," Akaar said, and to Asarem he added, "The *Gryphon* is looking into that possibility right now."

"Exactly," Ro agreed. "Once the murder was committed, we assume the killer would want to get as far from the scene of the crime as possible. But what if the killer *knew* we'd assume that?" Ro looked at Kira. "Think about it, Colonel: We had our shields up during the ceremony. The *Gryphon* was the only active ship in the system, and yet Gard beamed away. Maybe he could mask his weapon to the sensors and then scramble them to conceal transport, but beam *through* the shields to a cloaked ship in wait? I don't buy it, sir."

"Superior transporter technology is not unheard of, Lieutenant," Akaar countered. "Colonel Kira herself was once beamed off the station across three light-years. You have no evidence to support your conclusion."

"That's absolutely true, Admiral," Kira said, and then turned deliberately back to Ro. "But assuming you're right, Lieutenant, then your conclusion would be . . .?"

"I think Gard is still somewhere on Deep Space 9, biding his time, waiting for an opportunity to escape."

"What steps have you taken to test this hypothesis?" Asarem asked.

"I have DS9's internal sensors sweeping the station section by section, with emphasis on the most likely hiding places. Several of my deputies are conducting on-site inspections of some of the more difficult areas to scan, using tricorders. And Taran'atar is also searching the station, shrouded."

"Have they found anything?" Lenaris asked.

Ro shook her head. "Not yet, but on a station this size, with its labyrinthine design, it's going to take time to—"

"Ops to Admiral Akaar."

Akaar tapped his combadge. "Go ahead."

"Ensign Ling here, sir. I have Captain Mello calling from the Gryphon. *She says she needs to speak with you immediately."*

"Put it through to the wardroom, Ensign." All eyes turned to the viewscreen as it lit up to show Captain Mello on the bridge of her ship. "Report, Captain," Akaar said.

"Per your instructions, Admiral, we've just completed our sweep of the Bajoran system," Mello said. *"Our sensors have picked up a faint energy trail, one consistent with a cloaking device."*

Kira felt Ro tense next to her.

"Can you tell where it leads, Captain?" Akaar asked.

"That's just it, sir. If the readings remain consistent, we believe it'll lead into Federation space. To the Trill system."

Akaar looked as if he'd been struck. "Are you certain?"

"My first officer reported the findings himself, sir. There's no mistake."

Silence again, broken once more by Asarem. "What else can you tell us, Captain?"

"Only that the readings are dissipating rapidly, First Minister," Mello said. "But there may be time to follow the trail while it's still strong enough."

"First Minister," Akaar said. "With your permission, the *Gryphon* can attempt to overtake the cloaked vessel before it reaches its destination."

Asarem frowned as she considered her options. "Very well," she said finally. "But I want Bajoran representation on that ship. Someone who will observe what transpires and report back to me. General Lenaris."

Lenaris stood. "First Minister?"

"Prepare to beam aboard the *Gryphon*."

"Respectfully, First Minister," Akaar said abruptly, "I must disagree."

Asarem's eyes darkened. "I beg your pardon, Admiral? Are you refusing my request?"

"Not at all," Akaar replied evenly. "But I would like to recommend strongly that Colonel Kira be the one to join the *Gryphon*."

Kira's eyebrows shot up.

"General Lenaris is the senior Militia officer," Asarem said.

"And as such, he should remain aboard Deep Space 9 to take direct command of Bajoran operations here," the admiral argued, "where I will also remain to assist as senior Starfleet officer. During this difficult time, it is essential that we send a clear signal to the rest of the quadrant demonstrating the Federation and Bajor's unwavering mutual commitment, and our ability to work together from the lowest levels to the highest.

"Furthermore—and with all due respect to General Lenaris—Colonel Kira is experienced with starship operations and Starfleet protocols. In addition, she is still recognized by Starfleet as an active-duty commander with all the authority thereof. She is better equipped to *participate* in the mission, not merely act as an observer."

Kira blinked. *What the hell—?*

"First Minister," Lenaris chimed in. "With great respect, I have to agree with Admiral Akaar. Colonel Kira is the best choice for this undertaking."

Asarem looked again at Kira, who kept her expression carefully neutral. Akaar's arguments made sense, but she didn't like the idea of leaving Bajor at a time like this. And although she'd come to like Captain Mello over the last few months, she wasn't sure how she felt about being assigned to a Federation starship right now.

Asarem was hesitating, she saw. Akaar was certainly taking a gamble challenging one of her orders this early in the game and under the present circumstances. But he made a good case, which Lenaris himself supported, and Asarem was no fool. "Captain Mello, how soon can you be ready to depart?"

"Immediately, First Minister."

"Very well. Please be prepared to receive Colonel Kira and to set out in fifteen minutes." Asarem closed the link and addressed her listeners. "General, Admiral, I suggest you head to ops and work out whatever strategy of mutual cooperation you feel is necessary. . . . Lieutenant Ro, please coordinate with Dr. Girani. I want your incident report together with the autopsy findings within twenty-six hours. Councillor zh'Thane, I would like you to come with me to Bajor."

"It would be my honor, First Minister."

"Don't jump to conclusions," Asarem warned. "I'm still not certain anything will reverse my decision. But like you, I am not quite yet prepared to give up on what Shakaar—and the Emissary—both fought in life to achieve. Please be at my ship in ten minutes. That will be all. Colonel Kira, please stay a moment."

Kira nodded to Asarem as the others began to file out. She caught the look on Ro's face as her security chief left the room, wishing Akaar would ease up on her. But after Mello's report had so completely torpedoed Ro's theory, she knew nothing else Akaar said or did would matter. Kira suspected Ro must now be more determined than ever to go through with her resignation, even if Bajor never joined the Federation. *What a way for it to end,* Kira thought, wishing she had time to talk to her. Despite their initial difficulties—and their continuing differences—Kira had come to feel a mutual respect growing between them, and had begun to believe that Ro's posting to DS9 had been the right fit after all, for both of them.

The right fit . . . The words completed a circuit in Kira's mind about recent thoughts she'd had regarding her own life, and she leaned over for a quiet word with Akaar before he stepped away from the table. "Admiral, may I have a moment?"

"Colonel?"

"I just wanted to thank you for your vote of confidence in me." Kira said sincerely. "But I'm confused about what you said regarding my Starfleet status. My commission was always supposed to be temporary. I resigned it when I returned from Cardassia after the war."

"Did you?" Akaar said, and then shrugged his great shoulders. "We must have lost the paperwork."

Did he just crack a smile? "I see," Kira said. "Well. I guess that explains it."

Akaar inclined his head. "Good hunting, Colonel."

"Thank you, sir." Kira watched him go, not quite sure how to feel about the admiral's little sleight of hand. Still, she was grateful for the chance to take an active role in bringing Shakaar's killer to justice.

Alone now with Kira, the first minister sighed wearily before she spoke. "We share a burdensome secret, Colonel."

"Yes, we do," Kira agreed.

"After the near-disaster Shakaar made of the Cardassian situation, I truly considered exposing his duplicity. It would have ended my career, but it would have been worth it to prevent such a thing from ever happening again."

"I had the same thoughts," Kira said.

"What stopped you?"

Kira considered her answer, then shrugged. "Faith, I suppose. I kept telling myself it was all happening for a reason. Shakaar, the Cardassian mess, the Ohalavaru—and just when things were at their worst, Yevir, of all people, goes completely around Shakaar to forge a relationship with Cardassia outside of politics, an initiative based on faiths coming together for the greater good. And in the process, he brought the last of the Orbs back."

Asarem smiled grimly. "Yes, who could have seen *that* coming? Yevir actually made the politicians irrelevant to the peace process. I'm still scratching my head over it. To my knowledge it's unprecedented. I realized then that it might be the start of a revolution in diplomacy. And do you know what else I realized, Colonel?"

Kira shook her head.

"No one but a Bajoran could have done it."

Kira considered Asarem's statement and smiled.

Asarem breathed out again. "What stopped *me* from exposing Shakaar wasn't faith, however. It was fear. I feared derailing Bajor's entry into the Federation, because I believed in it. Now Shakaar is dead, and I wonder if I was wrong."

"Wrong about what?" Kira asked. "About not exposing Shakaar, or about Federation unity?"

"Both," Asarem said. "Shakaar was up to something. Colonel. We both know that. Something that was tied to his efforts to speed us into Federation membership. And yet he felt threatened by the Cardassian peace initiative, which could only have helped his cause. But now he's dead, with the result that Bajor and the Federation may never come together.

"So I now find myself wondering . . . which is the lesser evil? To complete what Shakaar started, when I know he acted ignominiously in his pursuit of it? Or to reject it, even though I know that a different evil may be attempting to pit us and the Federation against each other?"

Kira was silent a moment. Then she said, "Put that way, you're right, it's a difficult choice. But then I remember that whatever plot Shakaar was hatching, he didn't start the process of Bajor's joining. He merely used it. It was the Emissary who started us on this path."

Asarem chuckled. "Yes, that was quite clever of Councillor zh'Thane, wasn't it? Her reputation is well earned."

"But she did have a point," Kira said gently.

"Yes," Asarem agreed. "She did. Unfortunately for me, however, neither the Emissary nor Shakaar will be taking responsibilty for what comes next." With a deep breath Asarem stood, and Kira stood with her. "Report to the *Gryphon,* Colonel. This conversation never took place."

5

The crash site was a forest. From what little they could tell by the ship's sensors, much of the planet was going through an impressive period of biological gigantism, not unlike Earth's Jurassic period, 150 million years in the past, or present-day Berengaria. Huge gymnosperms carpeted the two primary continents, where myriad small forest-dwelling animals ran and flew. Sea life was also abundant—and colossal in many cases—but the most spectacular inhabitants of this world were the variety of towering, armorplated, multilimbed landwalkers that lumbered among the trees. The away team beamed down with phasers drawn.

A strong warm wind tugged at Vaughn's uniform once he materialized, pushing him back a half-step before he could completely steel himself against it. Clouds hung heavily overhead, with intermittent flashes of lightning. The wind howled, but strangely, there was no rain.

"Dax warned us the weather might be inconvenient," Bowers shouted over the wind. "But she seemed pretty sure it wouldn't get worse than this."

Vaughn nodded, squinting at the terrain. Visibility was poor beyond ten meters; the forest was dense. Neverthless, the Jem'Hadar wreckage was supposed to be . . .

"There," Nog called out, pointing toward a gap in the trees as he peered at his tricorder. "The fragments we detected start in that direction." Smaller than Vaughn or Bowers, Nog had to work hard to keep his footing against the wind.

"Let's get moving, then," Vaughn said. "Sam, maintain a scan for life-forms. We don't want to be accosted by a predator."

Wrist lights went on as the away team entered the gloom beneath the forest canopy. As they walked deeper, the wind lessened until they could speak to one another without shouting. They were almost on top of the wreckage before they realized it, and had it not been for the tricorders, they might have missed it completely. Half-buried in muddy earth, so much vegetation had overgrown the portions still above the ground that it looked just like a slope in the terrain. A bare patch of dark metal among the thorny vines was the only obvious indication the ship was there at all.

"Damn," Bowers muttered, and pointed. Next to the "hill," a flat, crooked tree stuck out at forty-five degrees. Then Vaughn realized his mistake. It wasn't a tree; it was one of the ship's warp engine pylons. The nacelle must have been shorn off during the descent.

"Can you tell how long it's been here?" Vaughn asked.

Bowers studied his tricorder. "From what I can tell, no more than two years. But I don't think—" He stopped and froze.

"What's the matter?" Nog asked.

"Life-form," Bowers reported. "Humanoid. Inside the ship."

"Is it the source of the transponder signal?" the engineer whispered.

"No," Vaughn said quietly, taking readings with his own tricorder. "That seems to be a few klicks southwest." He looked at Bowers. "How do you want to handle your friend in there?"

"We spread out," Bowers suggested. "Tricorder's showing an open hatch on the other side, facing west. You and I can approach from north and south. There's enough vegetation covering the ship that Nog can probably cross the top of the hull without making a lot of noise. Then we flush out the occupant."

Vaughn looked at Nog. "Are you game, Lieutenant?"

Nog swallowed, but nodded. Nog's fear and hatred of the Jem'Hadar was no secret, having had his leg shot off by one in a vicious ground assault during the war. His recent experience with the alien "cathedral" artifact had forced him to confront the demons that haunted him still regarding the Dominion's genetically enhanced soldier species, but any rational being would fear a confrontation with them.

"You'll do fine," Vaughn assured him. "Phasers on stun, gentlemen. Let's do this."

Sam took the south way around the ship, passing under the engine pylon. Working his tricorder as he walked, he tried to determine the exact nature of their quarry, but the vaguely humanoid heat signature on the display refused to resolve itself any further. Though Vaughn was eclipsed by the swell of the ship between them, Sam could see Nog creeping along the top toward the bow.

The moment Sam had walked far enough to see the open hatch, he stepped back, looking for cover that might also offer a clear line of sight of the opening. Ten meters ahead was a conifer wide enough to conceal him. Counting to three in his head, he bolted for the tree, staying low, trying to avoid snapping twigs as he went.

Safely behind the tree, Sam leaned his back against it and peeked out. He spotted Vaughn waving to him from behind another tree, twenty meters north. Their positions allowed them to triangulate on the ship hatch. *Perfect,* Sam thought. *Now all we need is Nog to bring up the rear. . . .*

Defiant's chief engineer was progressing slowly across the top of the ship, but Sam couldn't blame him for taking his time. Footsteps on the hull would alert the ship's occupant too soon. Better that Nog be slow and silent than to make noise in haste.

Sam took a moment to recheck his tricorder. The heat signature was still there, moving only a little. It seemed to be sitting on its haunches.

Suddenly Sam heard the sound of sand skidding over metal. The heat signature grew brighter, and began moving inside the ship more alertly. Sam looked out, saw that Nog had frozen in his tracks above the hatch. His foot must have pushed against some loose soil on the hull. It was sliding off in a steady, noisy stream.

Dammit!

Sam looked questioningly at Vaughn, who nodded. Checking the setting on his phaser, Sam flattened himself against the tree and called out, "Attention occupant of the Dominion spacecraft. We're from the United Federation of Planets. We mean you no harm, but we wish to speak with you."

Ten seconds went by. Then twenty. Then thirty. No one came out. Sam looked at his tricorder again, resetting it to detect EM signatures. There was no indication of any power sources inside, which meant no energy weapons. The chances were good that if he approached, he wouldn't be fired upon. *On the other hand,* he told himself, *a bow and arrow or a slingshot wouldn't show up either, and they could kill just as effectively as a phaser. There has to be a way to—*

Movement. Something big and green shot out of the opening and flew straight toward the forest canopy, lost almost instantly among the forest green. It looked a little like a crane. No one fired.

Sam checked for life-signs inside the ship. Nothing.

Vaughn stepped out from behind his tree, scowling as he walked toward the opening, where Nog was already climbing down from off his perch.

"Sir, I'm sorry, I really thought it was humanoid," Sam said, joining his shipmates.

"I was *this* close to shooting that thing," Nog said. "What was it anyway? A bird?"

Vaughn shrugged. "Look on the bright side, Sam. You weren't that far off. It was a biped."

Sam smiled ruefully. "Coulda sworn there was something humanoid in there. But readings are clear now."

"Then let's check it out." The commander tapped his combadge. "Vaughn to *Defiant*."

"Dax here. Go ahead."

"We've located Objective One, Lieutenant, and are proceeding inside."

Nog was spooked.

It wasn't even the wreckage of the Dominion ship that troubled him, although that had certainly had its share of creepiness. Moving through the smashed interior had been like navigating one of Uncle Quark's pleasure mazes in the holosuites, except that the surprise in the center was something out of a nightmare instead of a dream come true.

Nothing on the ship worked, so they had only their wrist beacons to cut the gloom. In numerous places much of the vessel's inner workings had broken through bulkheads, making a number of corridors impassable. Complicating matters was the tilt of the ship, which caused the decks to slope almost twenty degrees to starboard. Worse still, the hull plating topside must have ruptured, because steady trickles of water could be found in a number of places, streaming through much of the ship and completely flooding the lowermost decks below ground. The stench of decomposition wafted up through the deck plates into the upper levels, where small animals and fungi seemed to be thriving in the dark.

They had to cut their way into the bridge, which had been one deck above the level into which the away team first entered the vessel. Though the bridge seemed to have suffered less structural damage than the rest of the ship, it was by far the most grisly: Eight Jem'Hadar and one Vorta had fallen in a heap against the starboard side, presumably killed in the crash. Nog had spent several minutes just staring at a Jem'Hadar skull, feeling strangely numb.

As with the rest of the ship, nothing on the bridge functioned. Whatever secrets its databanks once contained were beyond recovery. But based on observations of the damage throughout the craft and tricorder readings they'd taken along the way, Nog and Bowers had agreed that the ship had most likely been shot down. Unfortunately, any residual energy left by the weapons used against the ship had long since dissipated, so it was impossible to say who their attacker had been. If it had indeed been a Federation starship, there was nothing here to prove it.

Vaughn seemed impatient, even restless. Having found nothing useful during their inspection of the wreckage, the commander told Nog and Bowers to complete their scans of the ship and to search the surrounding terrain for additional clues that might explain its fate. Vaughn would move on toward the source of the transponder signal alone. Bowers hadn't liked that idea, and said so, but the commander made it clear it wasn't open to discussion. That was when Nog's anxiety began to escalate dramatically.

It was difficult to pinpoint, but the longer they walked, the more Nog became convinced that something wasn't right with the forest. He felt like they weren't alone, that something was nearby, watching them. Bowers had continued scanning for life-signs, but found nothing unexpected within range of his tricorder. The nearest of the larger creatures they'd detected from orbit was to the north, kilometers distant. Locally, there were only small lizardlike animals, dense plant life, and a few green-quilled avians like the one they'd seen earlier hopping among the treetops.

But something else was out there. Nog could feel it in his lobes. A presence . . .

"Sir," Nog said to Bowers, "I think something is watching us."

Bowers surveyed the terrain and frowned. He tapped his combadge. "Bowers to *Defiant*."

"Dax here. Go ahead, Sam."

"Lieutenant, anything new on sensors?"

"Negative. Atmospheric interference is still playing havoc with our scans."

"How's our transporter lock?"

There was pause on the other end. *"Chao reports the locks are solid. Is anything wrong?"*

"Not yet. But stand by. Bowers out." He frowned and turned back to Nog. "How sure are you?"

Nog shrugged uncertainly. "It's just a feeling," he admitted.

Bowers seemed to consider that for a moment, then checked his tricorder one more time. "Still nothing. But let's assume you're right. What do you think you're picking up on?"

Nog squinted his eyes and listened to the sounds of the planet. After a moment he shook his head and resumed scanning. "I'm not sure. I'm probably wrong. But I can't shake the feeling that—" He stopped, staring at his tricorder.

"What is it?" Bowers asked.

"I'm picking up a large creature about two-hundred meters north," Nog said. "One of the sauropods we detected from orbit."

Bowers nodded and checked his phaser. "We'll search elsewhere till it moves on. Keep track of it."

"Sir," Nog said, "that's not the problem. When we scanned this area the nearest of its species was kilometers away. That animal didn't wander in. It just appeared out of nowhere."

Sam examined the tricorder log with a growing sense of disbelief. One second the forest area had appeared as normal. The next, as Nog had reported, the animal had simply appeared out of nowhere.

"A hundred and ninety meters," Nog said, his voiced hushed. He was tracking the current position of the animal while Sam tried to ascertain its origins.

71

"Incredible," Sam said.

"A hundred and ninety-five meters," Nog said. "Staying within a range of two hundred ten and one hundred and seventy meters so far, sir."

"This doesn't make any sense."

Nog took his eyes off the readout to look at him for a second.

"You know what makes no sense? That humanoid on the ship disappearing. The crane that flew out—now that came from nowhere. One hundred eighty meters."

Sam replayed the animal's appearance again.

"One-sixty."

Bowers considered the situation.

"The humanoid disappeared, and then the crane appeared. When this animal appeared, there was a crane in the area . . . and *it* disappeared."

The animal had advanced to one hundred fifty meters, but Nog said nothing.

"I think it's a changeling," Bowers said quietly.

Nog nodded. "I think you're right."

"It must have been on the Jem'Hadar ship and survived the crash."

Nog nodded again. "There was a Vorta among the dead on the ship," he said. "They don't always travel with the Jem'Hadar, but there's usually one around a Founder. Should we notify the commander?"

Bowers hesitated. "We don't have a lot to go on. And the commander . . . I don't think he'd appreciate speculation right now." He exchanged a look with Nog that said a lot more than either of them could voice aloud. The commander's behavior on the mission had been unusual, and Bowers liked a certain amount of predictability in a senior officer. "We need more proof."

"It must want something," Nog said, tracking it again. "It's risking detection every time it changes shape." He looked up. "It's definitely following us, sir. It's at a hundred meters now."

Bowers peered through the trees, but saw nothing through the dense forest. "It's interested in us. That's good." Nog's expression said clearly that he disagreed. "At least we don't have to chase it across half the planet."

"True."

"On the other hand, I don't think it's going to walk up and submit to a blood test."

Nog smiled. "Maybe not. But we know a phaser set at 3.5 should cause it to revert back into its liquid state—if it *is* a Founder."

Sam shook his head. "We can't just open fire on another life-form, even if it is a Founder. I don't want to make an enemy of it."

"The only way I can see to prove it's a Founder is to force it to change form," Nog argued. "We can't do that without a phaser. Sir, if it's been alone here for two years, it *is* still our enemy. I mean, it must think it is."

"Well, I'm not going to shoot it like a mad dog in the street," Bowers said. "We'll set a trap. When its curiosity gets the best of it, it'll have no one to blame but itself."

* * *

Nog scratched the back of his neck. The breeze was making him itchy, the forest smelled, and little noises were coming from all around—leaves shifting, animals moving among the branches, the cranes calling to one another in the distance. And now a Founder was out there, too.

According to the tricorder it was maybe sixty meters away, almost on top of the impromptu "base camp" he and Bowers had hastily assembled, and then just as hastily appeared to abandon. But not without leaving a phaser behind.

Assembling the trap hadn't been difficult, but executing it might be. The phaser had been set to level 3.2, against Nog's better judgment, and slaved to Bowers's tricorder, so that it could be triggered remotely. It would force a Founder back into its gelatinous state without harming it. But the creature wouldn't be stunned, either, and would undoubtedly take off into the woods.

Bowers insisted that curiosity would draw it back eventually, since it had been the only sentient creature on the planet for two years. Nog was also willing to bet it would come back, if only because this was a planet singularly lacking in opportunity. *The riskier the road, the greater the profit.* The thing to remember about other people's profit was, it inevitably came at the expense of someone else. And that someone could easily be Nog.

Bowers tapped Nog's shoulder and Nog jerked his attention back to the base camp. A large reptilian head had emerged from the thick forest growth and the rest of the animal quickly followed. From their vantage point up hill, the beast was smaller than Nog had expected—only five meters long, its midnight-blue hide covered in overlapping brown plates from nose to tail. Its four eyes surveyed its surroundings.

Nog watched as the creature advanced on the trap . . .

And . . . now! Bowers tapped the tricorder touch-pad with more force than was really necessary and jerked forward with pent-up excitment. From below them came the faint whine of the modified phaser and the animal jerked, too. Abruptly the beast shrank and altered shape, changing into an a morphous mass of gelatinous amber before coalescing into a new form—not unlike a smaller, female version of Odo. In another flash the girl transformed into a crane and flung itself up, out of the clearing, and flew unsteadily to the east.

Bowers launched himself forward and scrambled down the hill, pushing against tree trunks and rocks as he went to keep himself from falling face-first in his haste. With Nog right behind him, he scooped up the phaser and ran back into the forest, trying to keep the crane in view. The branches and uneven terrain were much harder to navigate at high speed and he tripped, twice. Beside him Nog was having a hard time tracking the bird on his tricorder and running at the same time. They had barely gone forty meters and were already far behind.

"Vaughn to Bowers."

"Bowers here. Go ahead."

"Is Lieutenant Nog still with you?"

"Yes, sir. We found a survivor. It's a changeling. We're in pursuit—"

"Belay that. Lock on to my comm signal and get to my coordinates, on the double."

"Sir?"

"That's an order, Lieutenant."

Sam held back a sigh of frustration as he stared after the fleeing changeling. He looked at Nog, who shrugged helplessly. "Aye, sir," Bowers said finally. "We're on our way."

Sam saw Vaughn from the top of the ridge. The commander was standing in the middle of a ravine, staring up at a cliff face where the ravine ended abruptly.

Wait a minute, Sam thought, looking at the details of the trench for the first time. The sides were far two straight and uniform to be natural. *All these young trees, this recent growth . . . none of it can be more than two years old. This isn't a ravine at all. It's a meteoric furrow! Something fell here from space!*

With Nog following, Bowers ran along the ridge toward an eroded slope where they could make their way down to Vaughn.

As they approached, Sam saw for the first time what held Vaughn's attention so completely. Something was buried in the cliff face.

"Oh, my God . . ."

Bowers's voice was scarcely a whisper as he and

Nog stopped when they reached the floor of the furrow behind the commander.

"At least now we know who brought down the Dominion ship," Vaughn said without turning. "But it cost them."

Gray metal plating covered uniformly with black conduits, metal struts and branching filaments, the hull of the fallen spacecraft faced them from its earthen tomb, silently testifying to the Gamma Quadrant's newest invaders.

The Borg.

6

Ro stormed into her quarters and threw her padd across the cabin. She knocked over a chair and paced the room, trying to rein in her seething emotions. Akaar, Asarem—all of them were wrong. She felt it in her bones. Whatever Captain Mello had detected, it wasn't a ship making off with Gard. He was still on the station. Every instinct she had screamed it. He would wait for an opportunity, when he was sure everyone's attention was elsewhere, and then he'd escape for real. She would need to post guards at every transporter and airlock. . . .

No, don't be an idiot, she told herself. *You were wrong. Get over it. Clinging to your interpretation when all the evidence points the other way is just foolish. It's better this way. Now you can resign without any doubt that this job was a mistake. Let the*

Federation come. Once this case is closed, you're out of here—

"Ro," a voice said in her ear. She spun around at once, launching a punch at the intruder—

Taran'atar caught her fist in his own hand smoothly, without even flinching. Ro shook her hand free of his grip and stepped back. "Who the hell do you think you are? These are my quarters!"

"I know," Taran'atar said. "I followed you from the Promenade. I needed to speak with you privately."

"I don't give a damn what you think you needed," Ro snapped. "I'm getting a little sick of your unshrouding right next to me whenever you feel like it. And I don't appreciate you violating my private space uninvited."

Taran'atar tilted his head slightly as he studied her. "You're angry, but not at me."

That's it. "Get out," Ro said.

"No," Taran'atar said. "I was monitoring communications from the *Gryphon*—"

"You were *spying*—?"

"Call it what you will," Taran'atar interrupted. "I do what I deem necessary to carry out my assignments. But I'm growing weary of the way in which everyone in this quadrant questions my actions. Do you want to know what I've learned, or are your moral sensibilities too offended by my tactics to listen?"

Ro narrowed her eyes. "Report," she said through her teeth.

"During my search for the assassin, I stopped to monitor all incoming and outgoing station communications from a backup subspace tranceiver in upper pylon one."

"You shouldn't even have been able to gain access to the tranceiver assemblies," Ro noted.

"Be that as it may, I did," Taran'atar said. "And since a stationwide communications blackout had been implemented for all but authorized transmissions, it was a simple matter to sift through the existing comm traffic. I learned nothing new from this . . . until Captain Mello contacted Admiral Akaar from the *Gryphon.* It was then that I detected a brief anomaly in the transmission: an echo."

"Meaning what?" Ro said.

"Meaning I was not the only unauthorized listener aboard the station."

"Quark," Ro whispered. *Please, no, don't let it be Quark.* She knew he sometimes hacked into the comm system. . . .

"No, not Quark," Taran'atar said. "I checked, and the Ferengi was fully occupied in the affairs of his establishment at the time. But someone else aboard the station was listening when Captain Mello was in contact."

"Then it's Gard," Ro said. "It has to be. I was right after all. He's still aboard the station." If so, she'd have to act quickly, before he escaped or did something worse. And there was a personal consideration as well: she now had the chance to make things right before she resigned. Before she turned in her combadge, she was going to bring Shakaar's assassin to justice.

"That's my conclusion as well. It wasn't possible for me to know where he was listening from, but there are a finite number of places aboard the station from which such a thing would be possible."

Ro went immediately to her computer interface and called up a station schematic displaying the locations of all subspace tranceiver assemblies—the twenty-four Cardassian versions that were part of the station's original equipment, and the six Federation models Starfleet had added after the withdrawal. *Thirty sites to check, scattered throughout the station. And it doesn't preclude the possibility that he's kept moving. But maybe there's a way to narrow the possibilities.*

"If you could tell someone else was listening in," Ro asked, "does that mean he could have been aware of you as well?"

"It's possible," Taran'atar said. "That may be why the echo ceased so quickly, and why my subsequent attempts to detect him in the same manner have yielded nothing. He may have gone off-line to avoid detection."

So he wasn't expecting someone else to be eavesdropping on station communications. He got scared. In his position, Gard would conclude he was better off remaining still than taking a chance moving from his hiding place. So how to pinpoint him? She studied the rotating schematic. Red dots glowed where the transceivers were located: the "antennae farm" right over ops, the lower core, around the docking ring, up and down the docking pylons, along the habitat ring . . .

Where would I go? she asked herself. *I just killed someone and beamed out to escape. But I can't leave the station, so I hide on board—someplace from where I can keep tabs on my pursuers, but where they're least likely to look for me. . . .*

Wait a second.

"Computer," Ro said. "Display detail on section 001–020."

Taran'atar leaned in behind her as the computer zoomed in on the coordinates.

"Enhance," Ro said.

The computer enlarged the area.

"Again," Ro said.

The image zoomed in closer.

"Again."

On the fourth attempt Ro saw what she was looking for. A small space, but big enough for a humanoid.

"Got you," she whispered.

Akaar scowled and cursed his luck as he studied the tactical display on the situation table in ops. Eight Federation starships were operating out of Starbase 51, the command base nearest the Trill system. He had planned to mobilize most of them to detect and intercept *Gryphon*'s quarry. Unfortunately, four of the vessels were on battle maneuvers in the Murasaki sector, too far away to do any good. A fifth, the *Appalachia*, was undergoing refit at the starbase.

That left only the *U.S.S. T'Kumbra*, the *U.S.S. Sagittarius*, and the *U.S.S. Polaris* available to assist *Gryphon*. Akaar knew that four starships should be more than enough for this operation, but he wanted nothing left to chance. He contacted the Starfleet personnel on Trill and coordinated increased runabout patrols on the edge of the system, just in case.

I have done all that I can from here, Akaar thought. *The rest is up to them.*

He glanced around ops. Everyone, Bajoran Militia and Starfleet, remained on high alert. Intelligence reports continued to pour in on ship movements and strategic operations throughout the Bajoran sector, as well as the situation on Bajor itself. But so far nothing suspicious had emerged that might shed new light on the assassination. There had been no claims of responsibility as might come from terrorists, and no strange activity within the Bajoran circles of power. Cardassia was being watched carefully as well, although its current representatives here on the station, Gul Macet and the elderly Cleric Ekosha, had been extremely cooperative in the security investigation. Nor had they, unlike the members of the Alonis delegation and several other visiting dignitaries, opted to leave the station once departure clearances had resumed.

Lenaris emerged from the station commander's office and walked down the steps into the pit. "The news is officially out," the general said. "First Minister Asarem has addressed the Bajoran people, informing them of Shakaar's death."

Akaar looked up. "What word on the public reaction?"

"Grief, confusion, uncertainty—and a lot of angry voices talking over each other," Lenaris said. "Militia HQ is receiving reports of demonstrations being organized by the isolationist groups, supposedly to commence in the next few hours. On the other side, the Vedek Assembly has come out in support of the First Minister's call for calm and her request that people refrain from rushing to judgment until all the facts are known. Councillor zh'Thane's appearance before the Chamber of Ministers and her interviews on the planetary newsfeeds have also gone over well. Advocates of unity with the Federation are planning a march on the Chamber of Ministers in Ashalla as a show of their support."

Akaar shook his great head. "After all my years serving the Federation, I still marvel that democratic systems work at all."

Lenaris looked faintly amused. "That's not something I ever though I'd hear a Starfleet officer say, much less a fleet admiral."

"Most Starfleet officers did not start life on Capella IV, General," Akaar said. "There, clashes between conflicting ideologies are resolved on the edge of a sword, or a *kligat*."

"General Lenaris," Ensign Ling called from communications. "I have Vedek Yevir standing by. He wishes to speak with you about returning to Bajor."

Lenaris sighed, but wasn't surprised. After instructing Ling to put the call on screen, the general looked up to face the hollow oval frame suspended from the ops ceiling. An instant later Yevir's face filled the frame. The Cardassian woman, Ekosha, was visible behind him. "Hello, General. Thank you for agreeing to speak with me. I know you must be very busy."

"My communications officer tells me you want to return to Bajor, Vedek."

"That's correct, yes. In the face of the tragic events we have just experienced, it is more imperative than ever that we work together to give the people hope. Cleric Ekosha and I will bring the recovered Orbs to Bajor together, and begin moving forward with our plans for the Vedek Assembly and the Oralian Way to exchange permanent religious embassies."

Ironic, Lenaris thought. *Yevir is willing to create a foundation for peace with another planet through its religious leaders, yet he's afraid of new ideas on matters of faith from his own people.* Lenaris looked at the acting chief of operations, Lieutenant Nguyen. "Next available transport to Bajor, Lieutenant?"

"Departing from docking port three at 0830, sir."

"Please arrange for Vedek Yevir and Cleric Ekosha's passage on that ship, along with their cargo."

"Aye, sir."

"Thank you, General," Yevir said.

"You're welcome, Vedek. As you say, this is a time when we must all come together." He allowed the real meaning of his words to sink in before adding, "Walk with the Prophets."

"Walk with the Prophets," Yevir echoed, and signed off. But Lenaris knew from the look on his face as he spoke the words that the general had scored a hit.

Lenaris had never cared much for Yevir Linjarin and his rigid orthodox pontifications on the Bajoran faith. That he had once been an officer in the Militia until a chance encounter with Captain Sisko changed his life somehow made it worse. Lenaris knew Yevir to be intelligent and sincere in his dedication to the spiritual welfare of Bajor, but it sometimes seemed as if the vedek had come to believe the touch of the Emissary had made his judgment infallible.

Yevir's spearheading the Attainder of Kira Nerys had been the final straw for a growing number of the faithful. Increasingly alienated by a religious leadership that had become mired in politics and conformity since the halcyon days of Kai Opaka, many of these Bajorans, including Lenaris, had recently broken away from the mainstream religion. Now they walked their own path, choosing to exercise the free will that Kira Nerys had sacrificed her place in the faith to empower them with.

Bajor was evolving, Lenaris believed. Not just in body and mind, but in spirit. And it was this fundamental idea that Yevir and his fellow conservatives seemed incapable of accepting—that there might be more than one true way to experience the Prophets, more than one true way for Bajorans to explore their *pagh*.

The thought spurred him to look at Akaar. "Admiral, there's something I've been meaning to ask you."

"What is it, General?" said Akaar, who had been watching Lenaris's conversation with Yevir without any obvious reaction.

"Bajor's religion," Lenaris began. "It can't have escaped your notice, or Councillor zh'Thane's, that a schism has developed among our faithful these past few months. Doesn't such growing internal disharmony work against our eligibility for Federation membership?"

Akaar tilted his head to one side. "Are you attempting to convince me the Federation should reevaluate its acceptance of Bajor, General?"

"No," Lenaris said. "But I confess to being a little confused. I had always understood that a planet had to be united before it could become a part of the Federation."

"Politically united, yes," Akaar said. "But no world—no union of worlds—is a monolithic entity in all things . . . most especially metaphysics," he added with a wry smile. "Besides—and this is something that frustrates many of my fellow admirals, but amuses me no end—Federation science has yet to discover anything—and I do mean *anything*, General—about the Orbs, the wormhole, or the beings within it that is in any way inconsistent with the Bajoran religious interpretation. Many of these things still defy the understanding of our finest minds. Who, then, are we to judge your internal debates on the question of Bajor's relationship to the Prophets? It may be that Bajor has much to teach us about that, and about many other things as well. That is our hope with every new world we embrace."

Lenaris considered that before asking, "And where do you stand on the question?"

Akaar looked at him and smirked. "I am a soldier, General. I stand with the people I took an oath to protect. Always."

The irony of having his own earlier words to Akaar

bounced back to him didn't escape Lenaris, but before he could fire off a retort, the illumination level in ops abruptly fell. The situation table and several interface screens went completely dark. Emergency lights came on, but the room was only a third as bright as it had been.

"We've lost primary power in ops," Nguyen said. "Auxiliaries have kicked in, but most of our systems are down."

"Can you get the primaries back up?" Lenaris asked.

"Trying," Nguyen said. "It looks like an override from somewhere. . . ." He tapped different sequences into his control interface, then slammed his hands on the console in frustration. "I'm locked out. We no longer have control of the station."

"Then who does?" Akaar demanded.

An electronic hum from the transporter stage gave him his answer. A figure materialized and took a single step forward, phaser in hand, surveying the operations center with a glare that, Lenaris thought, could melt neutronium.

Ro Laren.

7

Bowers couldn't believe what he was seeing. A Borg ship, here in the Gamma Quadrant—a region of space the collective wasn't known to have penetrated before. And if the evidence could be believed, it had clashed with a Dominion ship, to the destruction of both vessels.

Bowers had faced the Borg only once before in his career: during their last attempt to assimilate Earth three years ago, he had been the tactical officer on the *U.S.S. Budapest,* part of a hastily assembled fleet whose mission was to defend Earth from an invading Borg cube. In the midst of the battle *Budapest* had apparently been targeted by the cube for assimilation, because drones began beaming into key points throughout the ship. Bowers had killed two on the bridge before the drones began to adapt to the crew's modified hand phaser frequencies. The Borg were very quickly overrunning the ship, and Bowers had been too late to stop one of them from assimilating Captain sh'Rzaan.

Fortunately, the crew had gone into the battle with a contingency plan. At that time *Budapest* had been one of five test-bed starships for a new offensive hand weapon, one radically different from phasers and designed to be used specifically in situations when particle-beam weapons were useless: the TR-116. Essentially a rifle that fired chemically propelled metal projectiles, the TR-116 was immune to the adaptive beam shields that made Borg drones able to withstand phaser attacks. With Bowers leading an assault team armed with the prototype weapons through the ship, bullets from the TR-116s tore through drone bodies like paper. The Borg never knew what hit them.

How many of his friends had he been forced to kill that day because of the nanoprobes consuming them from the inside out, turning them into creatures of the collective? He tried not to remember, but the faces still haunted his nightmares. Jalarin, Hughes, Selok, Perez . . . Bowers had even looked into the pale, transformed face of sh'Rzaan as his former captain attacked Ensign Demarest, knowing he had no choice except to fire if Demarest was to be spared the same fate.

Budapest had won the day, but the cost had been horrific.

Now as he stood in the furrow created by the crash of the Borg ship, staring up at the broken hull that lay almost completely buried in the cliff, Bowers recalled that terrible day three years ago and found himself wishing Starfleet had never taken the TR-116 out of service.

Nog was walking up to the wreckage. Something had caught his attention. "Woah . . . Sir, this isn't a Borg ship. Or at least, it wasn't always."

Vaughn didn't respond. He seemed to be somewhere else. "What do you mean, Nog?" Bowers asked.

"The hull plating under the Borg technology . . . I'd know it anywhere. It's Starfleet."

Stunned, Bowers looked at Vaughn for a reaction. He hadn't moved. But then, speaking quietly, he said, *"U.S.S. Valkyrie,* Paladin-class, NCC-68816. Crew complement: 30. Lost with all hands stardate 46935 during a Borg engagement at the planet Uridi'si. Presumed destroyed."

Seven years ago, Bowers thought. Then the realization hit him and he stared at Vaughn. *My God, he was there.*

As if rousing himself from a dream, Vaughn opened his tricorder and pointed toward a narrow breech in the hull. "Let's go. What we're looking for is in there."

The transponder signal! Bowers had almost forgotten about it. Nog glanced at him, looking worried. Sam knew that entering the wrecks of two deadly Federation enemies in one day had to be fraying the engineer's nerves. But he also knew Nog had proven time and again that he was made of sterner stuff than he himself realized. Nervous he might be, but Nog would never fail to come through when the situation required it. Sam watched him steel himself and follow Vaughn through the breech, with Bowers bringing up the rear.

Once again relying on wrist lights to navigate the dark, dead interior, the away team half-climbed through the bowels of what had once been a Federation starship. Familiar corridor configurations had been transformed by Borg technology that seemed to have invaded every square meter of the ship. Unlike the wreckage of the Dominion craft, animals and plant life had not encroached on the interior of the Borg ship. Maybe the conditions inside wouldn't sustain anything long enough to allow life to thrive; it was cold in here, and there was an almost antiseptic taste to the air. Or maybe the animals just knew instinctively that they should stay away.

Nog narrowly sidestepped the inert body of a drone—a Vulcan, Bowers guessed, judging from the distinctive size of the skull—collapsed over a Borg interface panel near engineering. Bowers paused to see if there was any indication of what had been displayed on the panel when it ceased to function, but the surface was dark. Vaughn stopped for nothing, not even when Nog reported that there was a faint energy reading inside the engine room. They pressed on, past more Borg corpses and ruptured conduits, following the commander's tricorder.

Vaughn stopped outside a door. It still bore a label that read SHUTTLEBAY, but without it, it might have been impossible to tell what the room's original purpose had been. A labyrinth of corridors and catwalks lined with Borg regeneration alcoves greeted them as they pried the doors open. Most of the alcoves were empty, but a few were occupied, the drones still plugged into the ship's systems, their organic remains long since decayed within their inert cybernetic shells.

Vaughn ignored them all, his pace picking up as the signal on his tricorder grew stronger. Nog showed Bowers the reading on his own tricorder: another energy signature, very faint, but matching the one he'd picked up in engineering. The conclusion was obvious. Something back there was still trickling power to something in here.

Vaughn disappeared around a corner. Cursing, Bowers and Nog rushed to catch up. While they marched, Sam made some quick adjustments to his phaser, setting it to cycle randomly through different frequencies with each shot. He gave it to Nog and then made the same modifications to the engineer's phaser. If one or more of these drones suddenly came to life, he wanted to be as ready as possible. Every shot would count.

Vaughn had stopped in front of an occupied regeneration alcove down a long catwalk overlooking the gutted remains of the shuttle maintenance bays one level down. Wondering idly if the Borg had jettisoned the shuttles or cannibalized them for raw materials in their assimilation of the rest of the *Valkyrie,* Bowers heard his heavy footfalls rattling the framework of the catwalk as they reached the commander. Vaughn was passing his tricorder over and over the drone in the alcove, which Bowers saw wasn't decayed like the others. It looked dead, but showed no evidence of decomposition. A hairless chalk-white face obscured by invasive prosthetic enhancements was mottled with charcoal-gray rivulets, the telltale sign of a circulatory system saturated with Borg nanoprobes. Like its dead companions in the room, the drone was plugged into the the ship's power grid through its regeneration alcove, but a telltale light winking dimly by the interface port showed that power was still being fed into it. A thick layer of dust covered the drone and every surface of the alcove. *My God,* Bowers thought, *has it been here like this for two years?*

"This is it. This is the source of the transponder signal," Vaughn said quietly, his eyes never leaving the tricorder, as if he feared missing some vital detail.

No, it's more than that, Bowers realized. *He's trying not to look directly at the drone.*

"You mean . . . this was once a Starfleet officer?" Nog asked.

"Most of these drones were," Vaughn said absently. "Though only DNA scans will tell us for sure. This one, however, I can confirm without a scan." Vaughn snapped his tricorder closed and tapped his combadge. "Vaughn to *Defiant.*"

"*Defiant. Dax here,*" came the reply. "*Commander, where are you? Your signal is weak.*"

"We've found what we were looking for, Lieutenant. But we need Dr. Bashir. Have Chief Chao home in on my signal and beam him to these coordinates immediately."

"Acknowledged," Dax said. *"Anything else?"*

"Stand by. Vaughn out." Turning to Nog, he said, "Lieutenant, begin a tricorder sweep of the ship. I want to know if there's any indication of active subspace links to the collective. Then start scanning this alcove—its construction, its operation, its power source, everything. I need you to become an expert on Borg technology as quickly as possible."

Nog's mouth dropped open, but all he could get out were the words "Aye, sir" as he reset his tricorder and went to work.

When the call came from the bridge, Bashir allowed himself a private sigh of relief at the knowledge that the big mystery of the last few days was about to end. And none too soon. Separating his desire to know what was going on from his personal relationship to the ship's fully informed first officer had been difficult enough. On the one hand, he knew better than to ask Ezri about any ship's business that Vaughn didn't see fit to loop him into. That was Vaughn's prerogative as ship's captain, and Bashir wasn't about to make Ezri's role as X.O. harder by attempting to draw the information out of her. He wouldn't have succeeded anyway; Ezri took her transfer to command too seriously to let anyone undermine it, least of all Julian.

On the other hand, as *Defiant's* chief medical officer, being asked to operate in an information vacuum was a sure way to put lives at risk. He couldn't prepare for something if he didn't know what he was likely to face. The fact that knowledge capable of minimizing the risk to the crew was being withheld from him was troubling enough, but it didn't take a genetically enhanced mind to know that the continuing secrecy was itself contributing to a notable rise in anxiety among his shipmates. And that, Bashir knew, was dangerous. Anxious people made mistakes.

And although Bashir had only a rough idea about conditions on the surface, just knowing that answers awaited him on the other side of the transporter beam gave him a burst of energy that had him nearly running into the bay. He ignored the raised eyebrow Chief Chao shot at him as he bounded onto the platform and gave her the order to energize—ready, he believed, for whatever lay ahead.

Of all the settings he had imagined beaming into, the heart of a Borg ship wasn't one of them.

Though his mind intuited immediately that the danger must be minimal or the commander wouldn't have ordered him to beam down, nevertheless he experienced an instant of cold fear when his eyes focused on the distinctive technology surrounding him. Lit only by the away team's wrist lights, the ship took on an extra dimension of terror. Bashir had never encountered the Borg before, but he'd read enough reports, and attended enough briefings and medical conferences about them, to hope he would never have to.

Still, Julian's irrepressible curiosity had been piqued the instant Vaughn had started explaining the detection of the transponder signal, the away team's mission, and what they had learned so far. Bashir hung on every word, the whole time running calculations in his mind about the effect this knowledge would have back home. Even after several small-scale attempts to invade the Federation had failed, the Borg remained a cause for serious concern. If they ever got it into their collective mind to attack en masse, it was all over. Fighting off a single Borg cube had consistently proven costly; fighting off a full scale assault might not even be possible, especially if it happened now, with so much of the Alpha Quadrant still rebuilding its forces in the aftermath of the Dominion war.

Why the Borg had thus far attacked with only one ship at a time remained a mystery, one that had many of Starfleet's top strategists baffled and worried, Bashir knew. Some speculated that the advance ships were simply collecting data on the Alpha Quadrant's ability to respond to, withstand, and recover from their incursions, adding new twists such as time travel to each assault as a way of gauging the Federation's inventiveness. Add to that the Borg intelligence that Starfleet was amassing courtesy of Project Pathfinder, and an increasingly complex picture of the Borg was slowly emerging, one that differed considerably from Starfleet's initial assumptions about the collective, and that necessitated constant reevaluation. And that was precisely what had Starfleet worried: an unpredictable enemy was dangerous, but one they still couldn't comprehend was terrifying.

But a Borg encroachment of the Gamma Quadrant . . . that's a new twist. Bashir thought he was beginning to understand Vaughn's decision to keep the information contained among as few people as possible until all the facts were in. What puzzled Bashir now, however, was the revelation that he'd been summoned specifically to assess the condition of a drone.

Thirty minutes later, together with Bowers and Nog, Bashir found Vaughn a short distance away, sitting on the catwalk, knees up, hands resting on top of them. The commander's eyes were closed, but Bashir could tell he wasn't asleep; his forehead was creased in concentration, as if his mind were searching for something that was eluding him. *Fatigue,* Bashir suspected. He was about to pass his scanner over Vaughn when the commander spoke. "Report, Doctor," he said without opening his eyes.

"I've completed my medical scan," Bashir said. "The drone is a human female, age indeterminate. Approximately sixty-eight percent of its body has been replaced by Borg technology, including most of the left hemisphere of the brain. Its condition is critical, but stable. The alcove is acting like a life-support system, trickling just enough power to keep the drone alive. But that's it. In its current condition, the drone can't function, and it can't survive outside the alcove."

"Sir," Nog said to Vaughn, "I've finished my scans as well. There's no evidence of any subspace transmissions beyond the Starfleet signal coming from the drone. Any connection to the Borg collective was probably severed when the ship crashed."

Vaughn listened to the reports silently, then opened

his eyes. He looked, Bashir thought, as if he was struggling with a decision. Finally he said, "Doctor . . . Lieutenant Nog . . . you're both to begin work immediately on extracting the drone from her alcove without killing her. Then you're going to beam her up to the *Defiant,* where you, Julian, are going to reverse the assimilation and restore the drone's humanity."

Bashir looked at Nog, who stared back at him, stunned. Wanting to restore a Borg drone to its original state was a laudable goal, but under these circumstances . . .

"Respectfully, sir," Bowers said, uncharacteristically agitated, "do you think it's wise to expose the ship to the presence of functional Borg technology? What if—?"

"I've made my decision, Sam," Vaughn said, rising to his feet.

Bowers frowned. "Yes, sir. But the safety of the ship—"

"Is my responsibility," Vaughn said quietly. "And you'll do damn well to remember that, Lieutenant."

Bashir held his breath. *What in the world is going on here?*

Vaughn met the gazes of all three officers and said, "Until further notice, restoring the drone is the *Defiant*'s top priority. All other mission directives are suspended. Security is to be maintained, both for the protection of the ship and in order to keep this from as many of the crew as possible. Am I understood?"

Not quite all at once, Bashir, Bowers, and Nog responded with "Aye, sir."

"Doctor," Vaughn went on, "You'll find the drone's medical records in a subsection of Ensign Tenmei's medical file."

Bashir understood then, his eyes widening. "I see. . . . Thank you, Commander. We'll begin work at once."

"Keep me posted," Vaughn said. He contacted the *Defiant* and ordered Ezri to beam him up.

After he dematerialized, Bashir went back to the alcove, Nog and Bowers following close behind. "What was all that about?" Nog said almost immediately.

Bowers shook his head. "I've never seen him like this. Ever since he found out about the transponder signal, he's acted as if nothing else matters."

"And why would the drone's medical records be in Prynn's file?" Nog asked.

Arriving at the alcove once again, Bashir looked into the still, pale face of the drone with a new understanding of what was driving Vaughn's decisions. The knowledge made Julian feel as if he's just beamed directly into the middle of a minefield. All he could do now was hope that when one of them finally went off, as he felt certain it must, the damage could be kept to a minimum.

"Because, apparently," he said in answer to Nog's question, "this poor woman is Commander Ruriko Tenmei. Prynn's mother."

8

Ro flexed her fingers on the grip of her phaser as she surveyed the room. Seven duty personnel at stations, plus Akaar and Lenaris in the pit. *This would go a lot easier if I'd been able to lock those two in the station commander's office when I implemented the security override. Nothing's ever easy. . . .*

Ro tapped her combadge. "Taran'atar."

"Here."

"I'm in ops. Raise shields."

"Acknowledged."

"Lieutenant," Lenaris began. "You'd better have a damn good explanation for this."

Ro ignored him and scanned the ceiling with her eyes. Four dual-support pylons radiated from a central hub suspended over the situation table, obscuring her view of the ceiling above. *I don't spend enough time up here,* she thought. *I never really noticed the ceiling before. This is gonna be tricky. . . .*

"Have the room cleared, General," Ro said.

"I don't take orders from you, Lieutenant," Lenaris said dangerously. "Relinquish control of the station and restore power to ops immediately."

"I can't do that."

"Why?"

"Because you might try to stop me."

"Stop you from what?" Lenaris asked. "What are you doing?"

"Trying to capture Minister Shakaar's assassin," Ro said, marching past the station commander's officer as she sought a better view of the ceiling. "He's right above your heads."

Everyone's eyes went up. The ceiling, of course, seemed peaceful.

"For your own safety, clear the room," Ro warned again. "Now. This is going to get very messy very quickly."

"Lieutenant Costello!" Akaar's voice boomed. "Place Lieutenant Ro under arrest."

You predictable son of a—

"Belay that," Lenaris said suddenly. "Stand down, Lieutenant Costello. All personnel, evacuate the operations center."

"General, what are you doing?" Akaar said.

Ro looked at Lenaris. The general was facing Akaar squarely, refusing to be intimidated by the admiral's superior height. "I'm giving the station's chief of security a little latitude, Admiral," he said evenly. "Unless you intend to challenge my authority as acting commander of Deep Space 9?"

Akaar said nothing, but Ro could imagine his teeth clenching. He might really believe she was untrustworthy, insubordinate, and criminally reckless, but he was still wise enough not to make the situation worse with a power grab over her.

Finally Akaar turned to the ops crew, who stood frozen at their stations. "Well? You heard the general. Clear the room."

As the officers and crew exited in the turbolifts, Akaar turned back to Lenaris, who clearly intended to remain behind. "I am staying as well," the admiral said, his tone making it clear that nothing, not even if Bajor announced it was joining the Dominion, would change that.

"Suit yourselves," Ro muttered. She finally found a clear line of sight that afforded her a decent degree of cover: the column next to the operations station. She slapped her combadge again. "Taran'atar, I'm in position. Can you verify the target?"

A moment of silence, then, *"Negative. Security sensors still do not register the presence of a lifeform beneath the array."*

"I'm running the risk of blowing a hole in ops big enough to send the station spinning out of the system! I need verification!"

"I have none to give. You will have to trust your instincts," Taran'atar said. *"Or make a leap of faith."*

Ro shook her head, muttering, "You and I are gonna have to have a long talk when all this is over."

She quickly adjusted the setting on her phaser. "Gentlemen, if I were you," she said to Lenaris and Akaar, who were still in the pit, "I'd find some place else to stand."

As the admiral and the general took positions roughly equidistant from Ro along the uppermost level of ops, Ro raised her arm, pointed her phaser directly at the central ceiling plates and fired. Something flared—maybe a circuit bank or a power conduit—and Ro held her breath, waiting for the pull of escaping air that signaled a hull breach. But nothing was blown out into space. Instead, metal plating and subspace tranceiver components showered ops. Crashes and sparking equipment resounded through the chamber, some of the debris bouncing off the ceiling pylons and spinning in new directions. Akaar, the biggest humanoid in the room, had to dive and roll to one side to avoid being hit by shrapnel.

Silence fell. Smoke wafted from the opening Ro had made, and she strained to see through it. Gradually it thinned. Blackened machinery and the intact outer hull of the station was all she saw.

No . . .

She searched the transceiver compartment and the overhanging pylons with her eyes. There was nothing, no sign that a humanoid had ever been up there. "Do you see anything?" she called to Lenaris, standing by the transporter stage. The general shook his head.

"Lieutenant," Taran'atar said through her combadge. *"What happened?"*

Ro couldn't speak. She stood openmouthed, staring at the ceiling, unable to believe how completely wrong she'd been. *Again . . .*

"Akaar to security," the admiral growled, picking himself up off the deck. "Send a team to ops immediately."

Still staring at the damage she'd done, Ro let her phaser drop to the deck. There was a crash—

Something smashed into the situation table, shattering the surface and leaving a large depression. The impact made Ro flinch, and for a moment she thought one of the pylons had given way. But there was nothing there. It was as if the table had simply caved in on itself.

Or something invisible had struck it . . .

Ro retrieved her phaser and advanced toward the pit, stopping short when she was halfway down the steps, unwilling to believe her eyes.

Something flickered atop the shattered situation table. Then whatever mechanism had been in operation finally gave out, and Ro found herself staring at the unmoving form of a humanoid, covered completely in a loose-fitting red environmental suit.

Ro trained her phaser on the figure as she looked up at Akaar. "Well, this just got a little more complicated, didn't it, Admiral?" she asked.

Lenaris looked at Akaar, who was staring intently at the figure splayed over the situation table as he made his way toward the pit.

"What is it?" Lenaris asked. "Is it Gard?"

"Oh, it's him," Ro confirmed, looking at the unconscious face through the suit's visor. "But what's really interesting is his choice in attire." She gestured with her weapon at the red garment. "This, General, is an isolation suit. It provides the wearer limited life support and generates a very localized cloaking field, small enough to hide a man. The problem here is that Gard could only obtain such a suit from the manufacturer."

"Who?" Lenaris asked.

Akaar bent over to study Gard's prostrate form more closely. "The Federation."

9

This will work, Vaughn told himself. *It has to.*

He stood in the center of the medical bay, watching Bashir and his assistants begin the slow, complex task of disengaging sections of Borg technology from Ruriko's body. Nog had solved the problem of separating her from the regeneration alcove by connecting it to a second, portable energy supply. After that, it was simply a matter of beaming Ruriko, alcove and all, directly to *Defiant*'s medical bay. Nog continued to monitor his makeshift generator, which provided Ruriko with uninterrupted life support while Bashir and his med-techs, Richter and Juarez, went to work. Ruriko had yet to open her eyes.

Bowers stood by with phaser in hand, prepared to take action if the circumstances warranted it. Sam had remained unhappy about beaming Ruriko on board, and with good reason. Vaughn was taking a huge gamble.

From the moment Vaughn recognized Ruriko's transponder signal, he dreaded making the choice he'd faced inside the wreckage of the *Valkyrie*. Until he'd actually set eyes on her, he'd manged to convince himself he had the luxury of time. But really, he never doubted for an instant that Ruriko was alive; special ops transponders were wetwired into the nervous systems of their operatives. They self-destructed immediately upon brain death. For Ruriko's to be working seven years after she'd been lost could only mean one thing: she'd survived.

That Ruriko had succeeded in neutralizing Veruda's A.I. before it interfaced with the Borg had never been in question, nor what the outcome would be. She and Vaughn had both understood the necessity of his order to take the *Valkyrie* and pursue the Borg ship, just as they'd both known that the mission would cost Ruriko her life.

But she beat the odds. She made it off the Borg ship and back onto the *Valkyrie*. What neither of them had counted on was the Borg's apparent success in assimilating *Valkyrie,* and all hands aboard her.

This is my fault, he thought as he stared at her face. *I consigned her to this, as surely as if I'd stabbed her with the assimilation tubules myself. She's endured seven years of hell because I was never able to put her before duty.*

Strange, how easily the old emotions resurfaced,

even after seven years. He thought his reconnection to Prynn following his encounter with the Inamuri would finally unshackle him from the past. *I should have realized. I should have known that something like this was coming. The signs were there, the coincidences too numerous. . . .*

"Sir?"

Bashir had walked up to him. Vaughn pulled his eyes away from Ruriko's pale visage and refocused on the doctor.

"Her condition remains stable. Using records from our database on the previous attempts to reverse Borg assimilation, we've neutralized the most dangerous elements of the Borg technology, but we've had to leave intact the ones that are keeping what's left of her body alive." Bashir paused to allow a reaction from Vaughn. He offered none, so Bashir pressed on. "Something else you should understand, sir: the extent of her assimilation is far greater than anything we have on record. It's possible that in time, we'll be able to restore her human appearance, but she'll never be able to survive without extensive biomechanical help."

"What about brain activity?" Vaughn asked.

"There's some, but it's difficult to be precise, because of the Borg modifications. As best I can determine, she's in a coma. But it's impossible to know how much damage she endured after spending two years on minimal life support. I'll know more after we've returned to the Alpha Quadrant, where the proper facilities can be utilized to—"

"No," Vaughn interrupted. "You'll do the work here."

From the corner of his eye, Vaughn could see that Sam had turned suddenly in his direction. He'd overheard them.

Bashir hesitated. "Sir, please try to understand. I've done all that I can safely attempt to do for her under the present circumstances. *Defiant*'s medical bay simply isn't equipped to handle a case like this. Certainly not without replicators. The degree of mutilation alone—"

"We're not leaving orbit, Doctor," Vaughn said. "I'm not putting Deep Space 9, Bajor, or anyone else in the Alpha Quadrant at risk of exposure to Borg technology until I know it's safe to do so. And only after her mind has been restored."

"I don't know that I can do that."

Vaughn's eyes narrowed. "Well, you're going to try."

Bashir met Vaughn's challenging stare and held it. "All right," he said quietly. "But I want to be clear that this is against my medical judgment. And I fully intend to enter it into my log that your orders are putting this woman's life and the safety of the crew at risk."

"You're certainly at liberty to—" Vaughn began, but was interrupted by the worst sound he could imagine.

"Mom . . . ?"

Vaughn spun around. Prynn stood there, in the open door of the medbay, staring in mute disbelief at Ruriko's still-standing form across the room.

"Get out," Vaughn snarled, moving to block Prynn's view as he marched toward the door. "Get out of here now!"

"But, Dad—"

"Now!" Vaughn shouted, forcing his daughter into the corridor. "Mr. Bowers, confine Ensign Tenmei to quarters."

"Sir?" Bowers said.

"Do it, Lieutenant."

Bowers hesitated, but finally came out to usher Prynn along, who stared at her father in disbelief. "C'mon, Prynn," Sam said gently. "Let's go."

Mouth agape, Prynn shook her head uncomprehendingly at Vaughn as he retreated into the medical bay and sealed the door behind him.

"I think he's losing it," Sam told Dax sometime later, alone with her in the captain's ready room.

Dax frowned as she listened to Bowers's report from behind Vaughn's desk. News about the crashed ships on the surface, the discovery of the surviving drone and its identity, as well as Vaughn's confinement of Prynn had spread throughout the ship. "He's got to be under a lot of strain, Sam," Dax said.

Bowers nodded. "I'm not disputing that, Ezri. I can't begin to imagine what he must be going through right now. But you didn't see him down on the planet, or in the medical bay. He's lost his perspective. He's made it personal."

"What do you expect?" Dax asked. "Ruriko Tenmei is the mother of his only child. To find her transformed into a Borg drone, after believing she was dead for seven years—"

"This is about more than Commander Tenmei," Bowers said, raising his voice. "We've discovered evidence of a Borg incursion into the Gamma Quadrant. Our first priority is to report it to Starfleet. But Vaughn's even suspended transmissions to the station."

"This incursion is over two years old. We've never encountered any evidence of Borg contacts in the Gamma Quadrant before this. It may be an isolated incident. The delay of a few more days or even weeks isn't going to make—"

"Lieutenant," Bowers said, "this is the Borg we're talking about. We don't know what the hell they were doing, or when they might return to finish the job. And judging by the fact that the wrecks down on that planet went untouched until we found them, it's a safe bet the Dominion never found out that one of their ships encountered a Borg vessel. I don't know about you, but I for one don't ever want to have to face a Jem'Hadar drone. And God help us all if they ever manage to assimilate a Founder. We need to do something about this *now.*"

Dax was silent. She knew Sam was right. And as ship's first officer, the responsibility of addressing the situation fell to her. "All right," she said. "I'll talk to him."

Bowers sighed and nodded.

"How's Prynn?" Dax asked.

"Mad as hell," Bowers said. "Not just at her father, either. She's pretty pissed at me for refusing to tell her anything, and for confining her to her cabin."

"I'll deal with that, too. Anything else?"

Bowers shook his head.

"Take the bridge," Dax said. "I'll relieve you as soon as I can."

Bowers nodded and left.

"Computer," she said when he was gone. "Locate Commander Vaughn."

"Commander Vaughn is in his quarters."

Dax sat back and sighed, wishing she knew what she would say to him.

10

"Have you questioned him yet?" Asarem wanted to know.

Seated around the wardroom table and facing the viewscreen with Lenaris, Ro, and Ambassador Gandres, Akaar listened with his brow knotted in turmoil. Gard's capture, while a major step in solving the mystery of why Shakaar was assassinated, had raised a whole new set of questions . . . questions he almost feared to learn the answers to.

"He's not cooperating," Ro said, responding to the first minister's question. "He's obviously been trained to resist interrogation. He might even be resistant to the standard truth drugs. Unfortunately, we can't even try those in his present condition without killing him."

"The injuries he sustained were life-threatening, First Minister," Lenaris elaborated. "Dr. Tarses was able to stabilize him, but he reports that Gard will require several days to recover before he can be released. He is currently confined to the isolation ward in the station's infirmary, under guard."

"But if you have the assassin alive, there aboard the station," the first minister said, *"then what is the* Gryphon *chasing?"*

Akaar and Lenaris exchanged a look before the admiral replied, "We do not yet know, First Minister. Perhaps Gard's accomplice. If so, *Gryphon*'s mission would be essentially unchanged. It was my intention to have Gard interrogated again before updating Captain Mello and Colonel Kira."

Asarem frowned. *"And can you explain the isolation suit, Admiral? Can you, Ambassador?"*

Akaar shook his head. "Not conclusively," he said. "Not yet, at any rate. Starfleet uses isolation suits for the express purpose of conducting covert cultural observations of prewarp societies. But the technology is closely guarded. I have contacted Starfleet Command to see what they can learn."

"I don't think I need to tell you that this is beginning to look more and more like a conspiracy by forces within the Federation, gentlemen," Asarem said frankly.

"I agree, First Minister, that it looks that way," Akaar said. "But I am not yet convinced that that is what we are really facing."

"First Minister, I assure you," Gandres chimed,

"that my government utilizes no such devices for any purpose whatsoever. If there is a plot against Bajor, then it may be by a handful of rogue elements, but certainly not by the people of Trill or the Federation. If Gard—"

Gandres was interrupted by the wardroom doors parting to admit Dr. Girani. She looked pale and exhausted. *No,* Akaar thought. *She looks as if she has just experienced a shock of some kind.*

"Doctor," Lenaris said, "do you have something to report?"

"Sirs, First Minister, pardon my interruption, but I've finally completed the autopsy report on Minister Shakaar."

"And?" Asarem prompted from the viewscreen.

"First Minister, my preliminary examination showed none of this, but upon a detailed scan of the body, I discovered two anomalies that I cannot explain. Shakaar's brain and nervous system contained an alien biochemical, which I've now identified conclusively as isoboramine."

Everyone in the room looked at her blankly except Gandres. The Trill ambassador seemed stunned. "That's impossible."

"I ran the tests four times, Ambassador," Girani said. "There's no mistake."

"And what is isoboramine?" Asarem asked.

"It's the unique neurotransmitter that facilitates the integration of host and symbiont in a joined Trill," Girani said.

Akaar's eyebrows went up.

Asarem positively stammered. *"Doctor, are you . . . are you saying Shakaar was* joined?"

"He couldn't have been," Gandres insisted. "Only Trill can be joined to symbionts."

"That is not entirely true, Ambassador," Akaar said, pacing the room thoughtfully. "Starfleet is aware of at least one instance in which a Terran served as host to a symbiont, at least temporarily, and under extraordinary circumstances." The admiral turned to Girani. "However, if Shakaar was somehow joined, then there would be a symbiont in his abdominal cavity. Was there, Doctor?"

"No, sir," the doctor said. "Despite the presence of isoboramine, Minister Shakaar's abdominal cavity showed no indication of ever carrying a symbiont."

Akaar scowled. He felt as if all the pieces were there, but the picture eluded him. There was something familiar about all this . . . but what?

"However," Girani continued, "a microcellular scan of the *wound* did reveal traces of symbiont DNA. Or something very much like a symbiont."

"What do you mean, in the wound?" Gandres asked. "The wound was to his neck."

Akaar froze, the realization hitting him like a *kligat.* He looked up at the face of Gandres, at those of the Bajorans around him and the first minister on the screen, and suddenly he knew that everything about the situation had changed. *Blood of my father, not this. Not again . . .*

"Admiral," Asarem said, watching Akaar care-

fully. *"What is it? You know what this is, don't you?"*

"First Minister," Akaar said, "I fear that I do."

Akaar walked into the infirmary's isolation ward, where Hiziki Gard lay stretched out on a biobed, seeming to study the ceiling. His eyes didn't move to acknowledge Akaar as the admiral stopped at the foot of the bed.

"I will come right to the point. I know why Shakaar was killed. We found traces of foreign DNA in his neck. We also found a match in the Starfleet database. Shakaar was host to a parasite, one of the creatures who infiltrated Starfleet twelve years ago and attempted to take over the Federation. The same species as the creature that a joint team of Starfleet and Trill civilian scientists encountered a century before."

Gard said nothing, just continued to stare straight ahead.

"What are you protecting?" Akaar persisted. "Why continue this subterfuge?" Again Gard refused to answer. Akaar slammed his hand on the edge of the biobed and stepped around it, leaning in close. "If these creatures have indeed returned, then they threaten all of us. This is about more than just Trill."

Gard's eyes suddenly met the admiral's. "You're wrong, Akaar. This is all about Trill, from beginning to end."

"Tell me how."

"Why ask me? You know about the previous encounters. You have the DNA. So you already know the truth: outward appearances notwithstanding, the symbionts of Trill and the parasites are essentially the same species."

"I don't know enough," Akaar said. "How long was the parasite controlling him?"

"Months," Gard answered. "We believe he became infected at some point during his diplomatic trip to the Federation. Unlike most symbionts, parasites completely dominate their hosts. They don't even access the hosts' long-term memories. That's how your people detected them during the last incursion, but only after they'd already overplayed their hand. There are also subtle indications in behavior and body language, but these are more difficult to detect. That's why I was called in. I've spent many lifetimes specializing in the behavioral psychology of joined beings. I was sent to DS9 specifically to evaluate Shakaar, and if our suspicions were correct, to deal with the matter."

"But what did the creature want from Shakaar? What was it trying to do?"

Gard arched an eyebrow. "To take Bajor into the Federation. Isn't that obvious?"

"But why Bajor?"

Gard shrugged. "A new direction of attack, perhaps? Infiltrate the Federation through a single species? Maybe to manipulate the sociopolitical landscape in this region as a prelude to some grander scheme? Take your pick. The only way to stop whatever plan they had was to stop Shakaar from signing the agreement, but in such a way that Federation unity couldn't go forward."

"That's why you waited until the signing ceremony," Akaar realized. "But why was it necessary to kill him?"

"He'd been infected too long. There was no longer a way to free him from the parasite. To all intents and purposes, Shakaar Edon was already dead."

"Are we still in danger?"

"Oh, yes."

"You said you were sent to DS9," Akaar continued. "Is Trill behind this?"

Gard smiled. "That depends on who you ask."

Akaar turned away, emotions seething. Finally he spun back around and grabbed the folds of Gard's tunic in his great fists. "Do you think this is a game?"

"I'm growing weary of you, Akaar," Gard said quietly. "You think you're old? Believe me, you don't know what old is. I've died more times than I can remember. Next to me, you're a newborn. So don't think you can intimidate me."

Akaar slowly released Gard, but the two men continued to stare at each other. Finally the admiral said, *"Gryphon* is on its way to Trill."

That seemed to give Gard pause. "Why?"

"Captain Mello believed they had detected the energy signature of a cloaked vessel, heading in the direction of Trill. We assumed it was you, so she set out in pursuit of it." Akaar watched the shock seep into Gard's face. "But if you are here, then it begs the question . . . what is *Gryphon* chasing?"

Gard did not respond at once. Clearly he had not expected the news. *So the Jem'Hadar was right, and Gard had heard only part of Akaar's conversation with Mello*. "If what you're telling me is true, then you've all been duped. Captain Mello is being manipulated by the same kind of creature that controlled Shakaar. *Gryphon* is going to Trill for one reason: to retaliate. Not for the death of Shakaar, but the thing that was inside him.

"You have to stop that ship, Akaar," Gard said. "You can't allow it to reach Trill."

Chief Petty Officer Miles O'Brien tended to think of himself as uncomplicated. He lived life by a very fundamental rule: If something's broken, you fix it. And if his long career as a Starfleet engineer had taught him anything—from his time aboard the *Rutledge,* to the *Enterprise,* to Deep Space 9, to his current posting on the faculty staff at Starfleet Academy—it was that people needed fixing as much as machines. More so. Especially family.

So when Kasidy Yates had contacted him all the way from Bajor with her unexpected request, O'Brien didn't hesitate. Privately he was skeptical about what he could accomplish—after all, he'd only met Joseph Sisko a couple of times and had no special influence on the man. But O'Brien also had a fierce loyalty to Ben Sisko, his former commanding officer, and there was no way he would hesitate to do whatever he could for the man's family, especially after what had happened to him . . . and to Jake.

New Orleans was literally minutes away from San Francisco by shuttle—only seconds by transporter— and O'Brien still had months of accumulated leave time he hadn't used up. Once he'd explained the situation to his current C.O., Admiral Whatley— commandant of the Academy and another old friend of Captain Sisko's—O'Brien quickly put his affairs in order and returned home, announcing to his wife and children that they were all taking a summer vacation to New Orleans.

Keiko had been none too pleased at first, rightly anticipating that August wasn't exactly the most comfortable time of year to visit the sultry city on the Louisiana bayou. But once Miles had explained the reason for their impromptu holiday, all thoughts of the temporary inconvenience promptly vanished. Keiko arranged to take time off from her research, and the kids, Molly and Kirayoshi, both seemed genuinely excited by the idea of a visit to a new city. O'Brien pulled a few strings with some friends in the Corps of Engineers, and by evening the family had materialized on the pavement directly outside Sisko's Creole Kitchen.

Judith Sisko, the captain's sister, seemed as warm and welcoming as every other member of her family O'Brien had ever met. She also seemed to look on the O'Briens' arrival as a godsend, which immediately made him worry. Kasidy Yates had believed that hearing from one of the captain's old crew, someone who had worked closely with him and been a friend to Jake, might somehow get through to Joseph where his immediate friends and family could not. It was an idea born of desperation, O'Brien knew. Something you did when all the better ideas had failed. If the family had indeed put all their hopes on him, this could turn into a disaster very quickly.

O'Brien rapped on the door to Joseph's room. When no response came, he slowly opened the door and stuck his head inside. "Mr. Sisko . . .?"

Joseph, seated at his window as Judith had described, turned on O'Brien with a scowl. "What the hell do you want?"

"Uh . . . I'm Miles O'Brien, sir. Your son was my commanding—"

"I know who you are," Joseph interrupted. "I also know you're trespassing. I didn't invite you here."

"No, sir, that's true," O'Brien said. "But Kasidy Yates—"

"Is she all right?"

"She's fine, sir. She contacted me in San Francisco and asked me to pay a call on you. And your daughter—"

Joseph turned back to the window. "Why can't people just learn to mind their own damn business? A man has a right to mourn his son, and his grandson, in his own way. You tell my daughter I don't need somebody from Starfleet coming into my home to talk to me about my grief."

"But sir, if I could just—"

Joseph abruptly rose from his chair and walked toward O'Brien with a fist shaking at his side. "Didn't you hear what I said? You're not welcome here! Get out and leave me the hell alone!"

O'Brien backed away, and the door slammed in his face.

When he went back downstairs, Keiko and Judith were staring at him. No doubt they'd heard everything.

"No luck?" Keiko asked.

O'Brien shook his head. "I don't think I've ever seen anyone so angry. Is he like this all the time?" he asked Judith.

Judith shook her head. "Usually he just withdraws into himself. You saw the way he looks, Mr. O'Brien. He isn't eating much. He never leaves his room and hardly budges from that chair. He's wasting away. It's like his bitterness is eating him from the inside out." She shook her head and covered her eyes. "I'm sorry you were brought into this. But I was desperate, and Kasidy said—"

"Shsh, Judith, it's okay," Keiko said gently, placing a hand on top of Judith's. "We're glad to have been asked to help." She looked at her husband meaningfully. "Aren't we, Miles?"

"What? Oh, absolutely," O'Brien said, wondering what he could possibly say to a man who'd lost so much. And would he be any different in Joseph's shoes? Molly and Kirayoshi were everything to him. To believe you'd outlived your own children had to be the most crushing state of mind for any parent. Or grandparent, for that matter. *How does anybody re-*

cover from something like that? How do you move past it?

Move . . . ? Wait a second!

"Ms. Sisko . . ."

"Judith, please."

"All right," O'Brien said. "But you have to call me Miles. Do you have a replicator?"

"In *this* house?" Judith shook her head. "Dad wouldn't hear of it. To listen to him talk about it, you'd think they were the biggest threat to human creativity ever devised, especially to the art of cooking."

O'Brien smiled. "I'm not all that sure I disagree. But I need to get access to one."

"I know there's a replimat a few blocks from here. . . ."

"Perfect."

Keiko looked at him suspiciously. "Miles Edward O'Brien, what scheme are you cooking up now?"

"Funny you should put it that way," O'Brien said with a grin. "I'm not giving up on him, Keiko. When I was upstairs, he got mad enough to get out of his chair and slam the door in my face. I think I know how we can get him to come downstairs."

"But what good will that do?" Judith asked.

"I'm not sure yet," O'Brien said. "But it's a start. Lead the way, Judith. It's almost suppertime."

It was the smells coming from his kitchen that finally did it.

As night fell, Joseph's nose was accosted by a stench that had, in all the years he'd been a chef, never once darkened his restaurant. It was the smell of murdered food. Of flavors and potential boiled away to nothing. It invaded his room and assaulted his senses like a troop of marauding Klingons, filling the house with a reek.

And it was coming from the kitchen. From *his* kitchen.

With thoughts of exacting painful retribution billowing behind his narrowed eyes, Joseph rose from his chair and followed the offending stench to its source. At the door of his bedroom it grew stronger. At the top of the stairs it was even worse, accompanied by the sounds of conversation and laughter. As he decended the steps, the room fell silent, but the smells only got worse.

Joseph Sisko surveyed his restaurant, the faces of his daughter and her guests staring back at him like children who'd been caught drawing with crayons on the living room wall. The father, Miles, stood in the kitchen, looking at him over the top of a huge steaming pot on the stove. The only sound in the restaurant was that of the wooden floorboards creaking as Joseph moved slowly toward O'Brien.

"What in the name of all that's holy," Joseph said, "do you people think you're doing?"

O'Brien's eyes darted to his wife and Judith, then back to Joseph. "Uh . . . well, I . . ."

"Hi!" somebody called.

Joseph looked down. There at his feet was a child, a boy no older than three. He was holding Jake's old

toy alligator and smiling up at Joseph. On the floor
nearby, a little girl lying on her stomach and drawing
pictures on a padd stopped and looked up.

"Hi!" the boy called again, grinning at Joseph now.
He was beautiful. So was the girl. Such beautiful
children . . .

"Mr. Sisko?"

Joseph looked up.

It was the mother, speaking quietly. "I don't know
if you remember me, but I'm Keiko O'Brien. We met
a couple of years ago when you visited Deep Space 9.
These are my children. That's Molly on the floor, and
that one's Kirayoshi . . ."

"Well, of course I remember," Joseph snapped.
"What do you think I am, senile?" He lowered his
eyes to the boy again.

"Hi!" Kirayoshi beamed, and he giggled. Joseph
smiled. Kirayoshi started flexing his knees up and
down in a little happy dance. *When Ben was a baby,
he used to do the same thing. . . .*

Joseph's nose wrinkled suddenly. He sniffed the
air and looked up again, recalling what had brought
him downstairs in the first place. His eyes found
O'Brien and impaled him where he stood. With slow,
deliberate steps, Joseph walked into his kitchen, his
gaze never leaving O'Brien.

The pot was coming to a boil, the lid rattling as
foul steam billowed out noisily. Without a word
Joseph reached for a pot holder and pulled the lid off,
the stench at its most powerful. Joseph steeled himself and looked inside.

"Do you mind telling me," he said after a moment, "what in the name of heaven this is?"

"Err . . . it's corned beef and cabbage," O'Brien muttered.

Joseph winced. *In my kitchen . . . !* "This," he said quietly, "is what you feed your family?"

"What?" O'Brien said. "What's wrong with corned beef and cabbage?"

Joseph sighed and turned off the stove. He grabbed the pot and handed it off to O'Brien, then went to the sink to wash his hands. Toweling off, he reached for an apron and tied it around his waist. "Judith, go to the cellar and get me some andouille right away. Then head down to the fish market and pick up some jumbo shrimp—about two dozen."

Judith flashed O'Brien a smile and got up at once. "Right away, Dad."

Taking a large sack of rice out of a cabinet, Joseph said, "Mrs. O'Brien, would you mind going into my garden and picking two large red bell peppers? They're on the far left. We're gonna make sure these children of yours get a proper meal."

"I'd be happy to," she said. "And please, call me Keiko."

"Wait a minute," O'Brien protested as Joseph began chopping onions. "What am I supposed to do with this?" he asked, indicating the pot he held in both hands.

Joseph glanced at him briefly and then went back to chopping. "Did you bring a phaser?"

12

For the first time in years, Kira stood among Starfleet officers and felt as if she was in the camp of the enemy.

Just after the Cardassian withdrawal from Bajor, a newly commissioned Major Kira Nerys had been standing in the prefect's office on Terok Nor, watching as the first Federation starships docked with the station. She remembered that the sight had made her furious. Bajor's independence was only days old, and even though the Occupation was still an open wound, Bajorans were celebrating and savoring their first taste of freedom in half a century. After decades of oppression, the Cardassians had been forced out and Bajor was standing on its own legs—ready and willing, Kira had believed, to face the future on its own terms.

The moment had been fleeting. The arrival of the

Federation had felt like substituting one overseer for another—one that, like the Cardassians, came with its huge starships and vastly superior firepower to re-mold Bajor in its image. She remembered when the first Starfleet officers had swarmed through the air-lock in their black uniforms, looking around in shock and disappointment at the disarray of the station. She felt their barely disguised pity for the exhausted Mili-tia officers gathered to meet them. She recalled their disapproval for the civilians picking through the refuse that the Cardassians had left behind. And all at once Kira had known she was surrounded by her ene-mies. How dare they come here in their immaculate starships, in their impeccably pressed uniforms with their superior attitude and presume to judge Bajor?

It had taken Kira a long time to get past those feel-ings, to see beyond her automatic resentment of the Federation's presence. Years of serving alongside Benjamin, Jadzia, Miles, Julian, and even Worf, had helped her to understand that these people were her partners, her friends and allies—not her adversaries. They hadn't come with the misguided idea of helping Bajor become more like the Federation; they'd come to help Bajor help itself—and the distinction between those two ideas could not be minimized, no matter what the skeptics might say.

But they were all gone now. Captain Sisko was with the Prophets. Worf had moved on. Miles with his family had transferred back to Earth. Jadzia was dead, and even though she lived on, after a fashion, in Ezri, she, Julian, and Nog had left almost three months ago for their mission into the Gamma Quadrant.

Now, standing here in the main briefing room among the senior staff of the *U.S.S. Gryphon,* in the aftermath of Shakaar's assassination at the hands of a Federation official, all Kira's old feelings were back, full force. She couldn't help it. Those she had put her faith and trust in had betrayed Bajor, had betrayed *her.*

Easier to believe that than the alternative.

And you know damn well what the alternative to blaming the Federation is, don't you, Nerys? To blame yourself. Maybe the Federation murdered Shakaar, maybe not. But it was you who failed him. You failed Bajor. And if this really was a rogue action, then by letting it succeed, you allowed Bajor's entry into the Federation to disintegrate. Everything you worked for in the last seven years—everything the Emissary worked for—is in ruins.

And maybe that's even for the best.

"Commander Kira?"

Kira looked up abruptly, realizing she had let her mind wander. Captain Mello, seated on the opposite side of the room at the head of the meeting table, had called the briefing immediately after *Gryphon* had gone to warp. Kira had declined to sit at the table with the Starfleet officers, choosing instead to stand where she could see everyone in the room. "I'd prefer to be addressed as Colonel, Captain," Kira said.

Mello looked at her gravely. "As you wish, Colonel. I was saying that our analysis of the energy trail is still inconclusive insofar as the exact type of cloaking device we're dealing with is concerned. But perhaps if you examined the data yourself, you might see something we're missing."

"Yes, I'd like to do that," Kira said, her voice hollow in her own ears. "Thank you, Captain."

Mello let out a long breath through her nostrils as she regarded Kira. Her eyes moved to her senior officers. "We'll adjourn for now, and reconvene at 1400. Dismissed. Colonel, will you stay a moment?"

As the other officers filed out, Kira moved to the foot of the table, looking at Mello across the length of it. When only she and the captain were left in the room, Mello spoke again. "Colonel . . . what can we do?"

Kira felt the corner of her mouth lift, mentally thanking Mello for not asking something as predictable and pointless as *Are you all right? Gryphon* had been assisting Deep Space 9 on and off for the last four months, and Kira had always found the ship's captain to be forthright and direct. It was one of the things she had come to admire most about Mello.

"You're doing all you can, Captain," Kira said finally. "The Bajoran people are grateful for the cooperation of Starfleet and the Federation in resolving this matter. And I personally am grateful for your involvement."

Mello sighed. She got up from her chair and walked around the table to stand in front of Kira. "Colonel . . . I know the crime that's been committed can't be minimized. What happened to Shakaar—and to Bajor—is heinous. The first minister's murder is a blow to all of us. Tensions between both our governments are high, and it doesn't take a genius to figure out that Bajor may not want to join the Federation now. I don't think any of us really knows what the future will bring. Those concerns, however, I'll leave to the politicians and the diplomats. Right now I'm interested in only one thing: bringing the assassin to justice. We're on this hunt *together*," Mello emphasized, grabbing Kira's shoulders. "We're on the same side, Nerys. I hope you believe that."

"I do, Elaine," Kira said. "But as you say, we're on a course toward an uncertain future. No matter what happens, my people will never be the same again after this. *I'll* never be the same. And, more to the point, I've come to realize that this voyage could turn out to be the last joint mission between Starfleet and the Militia . . . and I just don't know whether to be saddened by that or relieved."

"I understand," Mello said after a moment. "I don't envy you your position, Nerys. You must feel adrift, and alone. But I want you to know that while you're on my ship, you're among friends. We're here to help, Colonel," she repeated, studying Kira's face carefully. "How long has it been since you last slept?"

Kira shrugged. "Probably too long."

"Nothing seems likely to change for the next few hours. Why don't you get some rest. I'll see to it you have complete access to our mission data so you can examine it at your convenience." Mello tapped her combadge and summoned her first officer back to the briefing room. When he stepped through the doors, she continued, "Commander Montenegro will escort you to your quarters. Anything you need, let him know."

"Thank you again, Captain. I think I would like some time alone. But if anything new comes up—"

"I'll alert you immediately, rest assured. Now get out of here," Mello said with a smile.

The corner of Kira's mouth lifted and she turned to go. Following Montenegro back out onto *Gryphon*'s bridge, Kira saw several eyes turn in her direction as she crossed the deck toward the turbolift. She was unable even to guess at the thoughts behind the looks she received, and that troubled her.

"Deck five," Montenegro said aloud as they entered the lift. As their descent began, Kira noticed out of the corner of her eye that like the bridge crew, the first officer was stealing glances at her. "Is something wrong, Commander?"

Montenegro started, embarrassed. "Uh, no, sir. I just wanted to say . . . I'm sorry about First Minister Shakaar. I liked him."

"Really?" Kira asked as the lift slowed to a stop. She suddenly recalled that Skakaar had fled the turmoil he'd orchestrated during the Cardassian negotiations by becoming Captain Mello's guest aboard *Gryphon* for a few days as the ship patrolled the Bajoran system. "What did you like about him?"

"His enthusiasm, mostly," Montenegro said as they exited the lift and started side by side down a corridor. Crewmen nodded to the first officer as they passed. "He seemed curious about everything to do with the ship. And when he talked about Bajor joining the Federation, his face would just light up. He even mentioned he was working on a proposal to allow Starfleet to establish a shipyard within the Bajoran system."

"Really?" Kira said. *A shipyard! When was he going to spring that one on Bajor? And what else was he planning?* "I had no idea. What else did he say?"

"To be honest, I didn't get to speak with him much. He spent most of his time with Captain Mello." Kira thought she detected a slight edge in Montenegro's voice as he said his captain's name, but it was gone almost immediately. "I was on duty when the captain showed him the bridge, and most of my impressions are from meeting him then. Ah, here we are." Montenegro stopped in front of a pair of doors and manipulated the touchpad next to it. The doors parted, and he gestured for Kira to enter.

The VIP cabin was enormous, bigger than anything analogous on Deep Space 9, whose accommodations were designed by and for Cardassians. Bright and luxurious by contrast, these quarters were lavishly furnished and softly lit. Vases of flowers filled the cool air with a sweet scent. Huge viewports sloped toward the *Gryphon*'s bow along one wall, and through them Kira could see the stars streaking toward her at warp. Nothing at all like the cramped, windowless, utilitarian cabins she was accustomed to aboard *Defiant*.

"I can't stay here," Kira said.

Montenegro's brow furrowed. "Would you like an upgrade, Colonel? I'm sure I could arrange—"

"An *upgrade?*" She remembered all the compliments she'd received during the last couple of months from visiting dignitaries to the station, remarking on Bajoran hospitality. But if *this* was typical of how they'd traveled to Deep Space 9 . . . "Commander, I hope I don't seem ungrateful, but all I really need is a bed, a workstation, and a head. All this is a bit . . . much."

Montenegro looked at her as if she'd just said the last thing he ever expected to hear. "I think we have something like that," he said hesitantly. "But it has a replicator."

Kira smiled. "I'm not a *savage,* Commander. Lead the way."

13

Dax signaled at Vaughn's quarters. No answer came. She tried again, and again the chime went unanswered. "Sir, it's Dax," she said in a raised voice. "I need to speak with you."

Silence again, which made Dax's frustration grow. She was debating whether or not to order Chao to beam her directly inside the cabin when she heard Vaughn's voice.

"Come."

The doors parted. She looked inside before entering. Like all the rooms on *Defiant,* the C.O.'s cabin was smaller in comparison to its counterparts on most other Federation starships, albeit a little larger than the crew's quarters on board. Vaughn was sitting on the edge of the room's single bunk, leaning forward with his elbows resting on his knees, hands folded. His uniform jacket was tossed over the chair by his desk. *He looks,* Dax thought, *as if he hasn't slept in days.*

"In or out, Lieutenant," he said when Dax hesitated a second too long.

Dax entered and waited until the doors hissed shut behind her. "Pardon the intrusion, sir. But I need to speak with you about the current situation aboardship."

"Which situation is that, Dax?" Vaughn asked wearily, lowering his head. He was looking at the combadge he held in his hand.

"I think you know what I'm talking about, sir," Dax said, unable to keep the edge out of her voice.

"And I think you've forgotten that what you're talking about isn't open to discussion," Vaughn said without looking up.

"Be that as it may," Dax said, "we're going to talk about it. Now."

Vaughn looked up. "Excuse me?"

"Sir, you can throw me in the brig after I'm done if you want, but I'm going to have my say, and you're going to listen."

Vaughn laughed quietly. "You think getting in touch with your inner Curzon is going to make me put up with this? You're dismissed, Lieutenant."

"Dammit, I'm not trying to be Curzon," Dax snapped. "I'm trying to be your first officer, and your friend. Or are you so wrapped up in yourself that you don't need either one anymore?"

Vaughn rose to his feet suddenly, staring down at Dax. "I strongly suggest you walk out of here now,

Lieutenant, while I'm still willing to pretend this insubordination never happened."

Dax didn't budge. "Why aren't we on our way to the Alpha Quadrant, sir?"

"I've already said—"

"The Borg have been here, Commander," Dax said. "They've been to the Gamma Quadrant. We should be learning everything we can about this incursion and taking that intelligence home as quickly as possible. Instead, you're making the restoration of Commander Tenmei our top priority and putting the crew at unnecessary risk. Why?"

Vaughn said nothing.

"You're the captain of this ship," Dax went on. "You have a duty to these people who have done nothing but serve under you faithfully for this entire voyage. And you have a duty to the Federation to put its security before personal considerations."

Vaughn's hands, Dax saw at the periphery of her vision, had clenched into fists. He was shaking visibly now, but once again Dax held her ground, and his stare. Finally he turned and flung his combadge with all his might at the mirror across the room. With a sharp impact the badge hit the reflective shatterproof panel point-first, and became imbedded in it.

The action seemed to cause Vaughn to diminish. His shoulders sagged, and slowly he sat back on his bunk, breathing heavily, staring at nothing.

Dax grabbed the chair, placed it opposite him and sat in his field of vision. "That's what this is about, isn't it, Elias?" she said quietly, using his familiar name for the first time. Even Curzon had never used it. "You've spent eighty years putting the Federation first. Every time. You put it ahead of yourself, ahead of friends, ahead of Ruriko, ahead of Prynn. Over and over. Now you're trying to make up for an old sacrifice."

Vaughn met her eyes. "I did this to her, Dax. She became a Borg because that's the situation I put her in."

Ezri reached out and took his hands in hers. "Tell me what happened."

"Everything?"

"If it feels right."

Vaughn let out a long breath, considering. Then, after a long silence, he started talking.

Kora II, Cardassian Union
2347 Old Calendar

Holding the small forcefield-isolator carefully, Lieutenant Commander Elias Vaughn moved the device in a two-meter-wide arc, like a painter making broad, unbroken brush strokes across a gigantic canvas. Hundreds of bright spots danced briefly along the incision, dying fireflies lining his makeshift bypass of the Cardassian security perimeter. Of course, the device couldn't actually slice through the installation's energized boundaries. What it did instead was mark the precise location of the intended ingress-point and relayed the data back to the orbiting scout craft. From there, it was a relatively simple matter for T'Prynn to distract the local security subroutines and manipulate the shape of the forcefield remotely.

Vaughn gazed upward into the chill, moonless night. One of the countless points of light that wheeled slowly overhead would be found on no Cardassian star chart. "Please tell me that Cren Veruda's brainchild hasn't detected either of us yet, T'Prynn," Vaughn said into his combadge.

The Vulcan's response was somewhat distorted, thanks to the scrambled comm beam. "I've detected no alarms thus far," she said. "However, I suggest you pick up Dr. Veruda quickly. I cannot keep the security systems occupied indefinitely."

"Acknowledged. Try to give me an hour. I'm willing to bet I'll only need half that long, but why take chances?"

T'Prynn's response was characteristically sardonic. "Prudent, Commander. As always."

Vaughn stood before the coruscating aperture he'd outlined and squinted into the darkness. Beyond lay dense stands of towering vegetation and an impenetrable communications shadow. Five kilometers from Vaughn's present position lay Kora II's artificial intelligence lab, the workplace of Cardassia's answer to Richard Daystrom or Noonien Soong. Other Starfleet operatives had cultivated a relationship with Dr. Veruda during recent months; they had learned of his conscience-driven desire to defect, and had discreetly worked out the logistics involved in making the distinguished cyberneticist an asset to the Federation.

It was Vaughn's job to cross paths with Veruda during his evening constitutional. And to get him clear of this place. Discreetly.

"One hour," Vaughn repeated. "Mark."

He moved through the aperture, heading toward the predetermined coordinates. The combadge was dead, cut off by the security system. Either he was going to return to the transport-zone with the defector in tow, or he'd never be heard from again.

Ten minutes later his tricorder confirmed that he had reached the predetermined spot. It also made it clear that Dr. Veruda was not present. *Damn. Something's gone wrong.*

Vaughn began moving back the way he'd come. He'd have to reach the gap in the forcefield in order to signal to T'Prynn that he needed a beam-out. The mission was a scrub.

A voice issued from his combadge, startling him.

"Hello, Commander." The voice was a smooth baritone, its inflections refined and cultured. Vaughn recognized it immediately and smiled.

"Dr. Veruda, where are you?"

"This isn't Cren Veruda, Commander. But you might consider me a close relative."

Vaughn's heart sank. He knew he was conversing with Veruda's A.I.

A proximity alarm light flashed on the tricorder. A trio of flesh-and-blood pursuers was suddenly on his tail. He broke into a run.

"Don't exert yourself, Mr. Vaughn," said the A.I. "There really isn't any point."

Vaughn pumped his legs harder. By the time he'd gotten within thirty meters from his entry point, he was feeling each and every one of his seventy-two years.

The night-visor betrayed a flash of movement in the shadows to his right. Without hesitation he fired, then heard a body crash into the darkened foliage, so much dead weight. Seconds later he dispatched a second pursuer who had come from the opposite direction.

A disruptor bolt struck him between the shoulder blades a moment afterward. *It's always the one you didn't see that gets you,* Vaughn thought just before the darkness of the jungle became absolute.

A voice drifted to him from the darkness. "Elias Vaughn. Starfleet special operative. Rank of lieutenant commander."

Vaughn opened his eyes and regarded the Cardassian glinn who stood before him. The Cardassian glanced down at a padd before turning his intense gaze back on Vaughn, who noted that he was lying on a table, restrained either by a forcefield or drugs. Looking down at his body with great effort, Vaughn saw that he was stripped to the skin, his black stealth uniform and body armor gone. The slight motion made his head flare with pain. *Disruptor hangover,* he thought as his memory of recent events returned.

He recalled the mission. The chase through the wilderness of Kora II after failing to find Dr. Veruda. The Cardassians knew about the defection. The scientist, Vaughn reflected, was more than likely already dead.

The glinn was regarding him with a look of patient expectation.

"You've saved me the trouble," Vaughn said, "of telling you my name, rank, and serial number."

The glinn laughed, a dry, brittle sound. But his eyes were hard, set deeply beneath gray, scaly brows. Vaughn could see at once that this was a man who was accustomed to getting what he wanted. He clearly didn't have to raise his voice very often.

This won't make for the sort of after-action report Ruriko Tenmei is used to reading, he thought, fighting down an absurd impulse to laugh. *But at least she'll find this particular mission hard to top. Too bad I never got to meet her face-to-face.*

But this wasn't the time to ponder the friendly rivalries so common within Starfleet's intelligence community. As long as he was drawing breath, the first order of business had to be survival.

"And whom do I have the pleasure of addressing?" Vaughn said.

The Cardassian smiled ambiguously. "You may address me as Glinn Madred."

"I hope you'll forgive me for failing to salute," Vaughn said. *Come on, T'Prynn. Find a way to beam me out of here.*

"We know that Starfleet Intelligence has been in communication with Cren Veruda for some time," Madred said, ignoring Vaughn's impertinence. "And that the good doctor has expressed a desire to seek his fortunes in the Federation."

"Really. Then maybe it's lucky that I happened to be in the neighborhood."

A door slid open on the opposite side of the room, and a slim Cardassian woman of perhaps thirty-five years entered. Despite her neck and forehead scales and ashen skin, she struck Vaughn as stunningly attractive. But one look at her hard expression convinced him that she would be a far less forgiving interviewer than the glinn.

That impression was reinforced by the symbol of the Cardassian Obsidian Order on her gray uniform collar. Vaughn suddenly understood why Madred saw no need to raise his voice. He was leaving the prosaic chores of interrogation to less gentle hands.

"I would like you to meet your opposite number in the Cardassian intelligence service," said Madred, bowing slightly toward the woman, whose almond-shaped eyes were fixed upon Vaughn's.

"My name is Kree Omiturin," she said. "Recently transferred to this evil-smelling backwater from Cardassia Prime." Nemeti's bitter tone made it plain that she regarded her current assignment as a demotion. And there was something else about her, too. . . .

"Operative Omiturin will, ah, begin interviewing you shortly," Madred said. "It's always best to leave information extraction to the experts, don't you think?"

"I think you're selling yourself short, Madred," Vaughn said. "I'm sure you have the makings of a fine torturer."

"You and another Federation operative have come to this world hoping to spirit Dr. Veruda away," Omiturin said.

146

Vaughn carefully blanked his face, well aware that she was scrutinizing him for his reactions. If the Cardassians had succeeded in killing or capturing T'Prynn, then he wasn't about to give this woman the satisfaction of appearing surprised. Perhaps she was only fishing, with no actual knowledge of his colleagues in the field. He fervently hoped that this was the case.

The Cardassian woman continued. "What you've failed to understand, Mr. Vaughn, is that you've arrived too late to protect your people from Dr. Veruda's invention. His artificial intelligence nodes are about to link up across the Cardassian Union and beyond via subspace relays. We'll soon be in a position to mount and control an assault against the Federation the likes of which you can scarcely imagine."

Madred cut in, his eyes narrowing in Vaughn's direction. "Unfortunately for you, the good doctor's expertise in devising countermeasures to his own creation will not be forthcoming."

"I want to spend some time with the prisoner now," Omiturin said, clearly not fond of being interrupted. "Alone." Madred nodded impassively before exiting. Vaughn found himself alone in the room with the flint-eyed woman, his body still immobile as he contemplated the remaining hours of his life.

Now would be a good time to get me the hell out of here, T'Prynn. Assuming you're still alive.

Omiturin approached the table on which he lay, studying him in silence. A hypospray was in her hand, as though conjured out of thin air. With surpris-

147

ing gentleness, she touched it to his neck. He listened to its contents hiss home.

"This will restore your mobility. And you'll find a prison coverall in the locker beside the door. Put it on."

Vaughn rose to a sitting position and got his legs unsteadily beneath him. The metal floor felt as cold as space against his bare feet.

She tossed him a Starfleet hand phaser. He caught it after bobbling it between his hands momentarily.

"I certainly felt naked without this," he said, sparing a second to check the weapon's charge before moving to the locker.

"Hurry," she said as she made for the door.

"Why are you doing this?" Vaughn said, studying Omiturin's hard, scaly features as they walked purposefully down the empty hallway. It was a relief to be clothed again, even if only in prison garb.

She smiled enigmatically. "If you're as smart and resourceful as your after-action reports paint you, then I'm sure you'll work it out on your own soon enough."

Vaughn wasn't surprised that the Cardassians had accessed his files. She was in the intelligence business, after all, just as he was.

"You forgot lucky," he said. "Sometimes luck is an operative's most important asset."

"Really. With superstitions like that, it's remarkable that you've made it to such an advanced age."

"Ouch," he said, returning her smile. "But my 'advanced age' tends to prove my point."

Omiturin and Vaughn came to a stop outside an isolated holding cell at the end of a sterile, limestone-walled corridor. She typed a brief command sequence into the wall keypad, and the forcefield dropped in response. She entered the cell, prompting Vaughn to follow. On the floor in the far corner sat a slightly built elderly Cardassian man attired in a simple maroon prison coverall. Vaughn recognized him immediately.

Cren Veruda.

The cyberneticist looked up at them with rheumy eyes. "Is it time for another interview already?" His voice sounded like an older, defeated version of the A.I. that had taunted Vaughn shortly before his capture.

"No more interrogations today, Doctor," Omiturin said.

Vaughn crouched beside the stick-thin scientist and gently helped him to his feet. "Easy, Doctor. I'm a Starfleet officer, and I'm getting you out of here."

Veruda seemed to become more fully alert. "Ah. The Federation man. You came for me after all. When the Order discovered my plan to defect, I'd given up hope."

"Hope's the easy part," Vaughn said, turning his gaze to Nemeti. "What's hard is escaping undetected from a high-security Cardassian scientific research facility. Any thoughts on that, Ms. Omiturin?"

"I've got the security A.I. in diagnostic mode, and it'll stay that way for another ninety-eight minutes. We have that long to reach the defense perimeter. Can your Lieutenant Commander T'Prynn beam us out from there?"

Vaughn nodded. "If she hasn't been captured."

"You needn't worry about that," she said as the trio

moved down the corridor, apparently a hardened Cardassian officer conducting a pair of prisoners toward some unpleasant fate or other.

After evading four regular security patrols in and around the complex, the group entered the verdant jungle, shielding their eyes from the blazing sun. Although the terrain looked different in the dazzling light, Vaughn realized that they had reached the limit of the base's security perimeter.

"You're not really with the Order, are you?" Vaughn said as Omiturin opened a gap in the perimeter forcefield. "I'll bet you're not even a Cardassian."

That seemed to rattle her for a second. But only for a second. She was good, but not perfect.

Moments later a transporter beam swept over him, and Vaughn found himself standing on the pads beside the two Cardassians.

T'Prynn swiveled her cockpit chair in order to face the transporter pads at the rear of the craft. Regarding the group impassively, she said, "It's good to have you back, Commander Vaughn. I have already laid in and executed a course back to Federation space."

Omiturin responded before Vaughn could get his mouth open. "Good work, Commander T'Prynn," she said. "If you'll excuse me, I need to escort Dr. Veruda aft. He needs to rest. We can debrief later." The two Cardassians disappeared behind the scout vessel's aft partition, leaving Vaughn standing on the transporter pad, scowling.

T'Prynn rose and approached him. "You appear to have something to say."

"You knew about this, didn't you?" Vaughn said, hiking a thumb aftward.

"I was aware that a surgically disguised Starfleet operative had infiltrated the Kora II facility's security contingent. Yes."

Vaughn decided that Vulcan Starfleet officers must have to take classes in Exasperating Behavior before receiving their commissions. It just couldn't be a natural talent.

"And you didn't see fit to reveal that fact to me?" he said.

"We both knew that there was a significant nonzero probability that you would be captured. Had you been told of the presence of a third operative, you might have been made to reveal that knowledge under interrogation."

Vaughn's pique began to recede, at least where his Vulcan associate was concerned. "You wound me, T'Prynn. Do you really think I'd crack so easily?"

"You *are* only human." T'Prynn wore the only expression in her repertoire that even vaguely resembled a smile.

Vaughn ignored the good-natured jab. "You and I have worked together on and off for, what, thirty years now?"

"It has been twenty-eight years, nine months, and sixteen days since our first covert mission together."

Vaughn offered her an *I'll-take-your-word-for-it* nod. "I can understand why my lack of a 'need to know' might be mission critical. What I don't understand is why the brass hats in Command sent *her* of all people." He gestured toward the aft compartment.

T'Prynn raised a quizzical eyebrow. "I don't understand."

" 'Kree Omiturin,' " Vaughn said. "Come on, T'Prynn. Don't tell me you haven't figured it out. It's an anagram for *Ruriko Tenmei.*"

T'Prynn nodded. "Ah. Your nemesis."

"Please. She's a colleague. I've made a habit of keeping up with her missions over the last few years. And she's sent me messages now and then assuring me that she's been returning the favor."

"But you had never actually met her before today." Vaughn nodded.

"Then I believe I understand your frustration, Elias," T'Prynn said, folding her arms. "At least in part."

Vaughn saw that she was still puzzling over something. "Which part isn't clear?"

"The source of your anger. Are you upset with Starfleet for assigning Lieutenant Commander Tenmei to this mission without your prior knowledge? Or do you resent being rescued by your biggest rival within the bureau—and on your very first meeting?"

He turned those notions over and over for a protracted moment before answering. "Those are excellent questions," he said at length.

T'Prynn was clearly not finished making probing observations. "She infuriates you."

"Yes."

"Irritates you."

"Yes."

"Exasperates you."

"Yes!"

"You are attracted to her."

"Is it that obvious?"

U.S.S. T'Plana-Hath
2349 Old Calendar

The Ktarian freebooter vessel had already exploded, vaporized as though plunged into the heart of a sun. Vaughn couldn't spare a moment to admire the spectacular blast.

He still had to make sure that T'Prynn got back aboard the *T'Plana-Hath* safely.

Why did T'Prynn always insist on cutting her escapes so fine? Vaughn thought it was a positively non-Vulcan characteristic. *But she always gets the job done,* he reminded himself as he extended the console's buffer memory and attempted once again to energize the transporter.

"Her pattern has degraded by sixty-two percent," Ruriko said. She stood at his side, her hands steadier than her voice as she bridged emergency power to the targeting scanners.

Had anybody ever survived such massive signal degradation during transport? Vaughn wasn't sure. He had to count on hope—and on the system's multiply-redundant holographic memory matrices.

"Again." They both touched buttons in a flurry of motion. Indicators and telltales flashed. The console whined. The transporter cycled.

Again, nothing.

We're not giving up on you, T'Prynn.

The transporter made strained noises that Vaughn had rarely heard before. A film of greenish organic residue fell from a dissipating column of light, splashing across four of the pads.

Vaughn froze, gazing in Ruriko's direction. Her huge eyes held the thought that he couldn't give voice to.

T'Prynn was gone.

Mount Selaya, Vulcan
2349 Old Calendar

Conducted by several robed masters under the watchful eye of T'Rukh, Vulcan's barren co-orbital world, the internment ceremony had been befittingly solemn. Vaughn also found the entire affair to be parsimonious and efficient. T'Prynn would have been pleased. Judging from the stoic expressions borne by the dozens of assembled family members and colleagues, it was easy to believe that Vulcans entirely lacked the concept of mourning.

Thanks to his long association with T'Prynn, Vaughn knew better.

Ruriko squeezed his hand tightly throughout the brief ceremony. She looked diminished, smaller in some way. Vaughn didn't try to restrain the tears that rolled down his cheeks as the vial that contained T'Prynn's mortal remains was interred in a family crypt beneath the ruddy, sunbaked sands of Gol.

After the funeral party and the guests had dispersed, Vaughn and Ruriko walked along a flat expanse of red-and-ocher Vulcan desert, watching the sun grow huge and orange as it began to sink over the horizon.

The sunset painted the sky with every color on the pallet from scarlet to salmon to deep purple.

It wasn't until an hour after the planet had slipped into night's embrace that Vaughn noticed that he and Ruriko were still holding hands.

Together, they looked up at the eternal stars. In his mind's eye Vaughn saw T'Prynn raise an ironic eyebrow. Had she been standing here, Vaughn thought, she might be tempted to comment that he and Ruriko would make a lovely couple.

Vaughn turned from the stars and looked into Ruriko's eyes. She was watching him expectantly. *Damn,* Vaughn thought. *It's always the one you didn't see that gets you.*

San Francisco, Earth
2349 Calendar

Vaughn and Ruriko returned to Starfleet Headquarters for a day-long debriefing session immediately after their return from the Monac System. They had delivered Veruda's computer worm, on target and on schedule. The countermeasure program—three years in the making, following the defection of Dr. Cren Veruda to the Federation—had entered the Cardassian grid at the Monac shipbuilding facility and had propagated itself via subspace relays before anyone detected it. As far as Starfleet's premiere A.I. experts could determine, the artificial intelligence with which the Cardassian Union had been tying together its offensive and defensive capabilities was now completely inert.

Three years fraught with a series of difficult assignments now culminated in this balmy San Francisco Sunday afternoon. And Vaughn found himself—astonishingly—with nothing to do except stroll through the Golden Gate Park Arboretum, Ruriko at his side.

Ruriko paused to admire a rhododendron nearly as large as her head. She closed her eyes as she inhaled the flower's fragrance. Vaughn smiled, admiring her long black hair, her delicate porcelain complexion. It was hard to believe that the first time he had met her she had been surgically altered to pass as a Cardassian torturer.

How things change.

Ruriko straightened and gazed deeply into his eyes. As though she'd read his mind, she said, "I've come to a decision, Elias. I'm not taking any more field assignments. At least for a while. I want to get back into nanotech research full time."

She regarded him expectantly. Did she hope he might drop out of the field as well? It certainly would make sense; he was nearly twice her age, after all. But Vaughn wasn't certain he knew *how* to quit.

"Is this about what happened to T'Prynn on the Ktarian mission?" Vaughn asked.

She nodded. "It's sobering to get a demonstration about how vulnerable we all are. That even Vulcans aren't immortal."

"She knew the risks. We all do, or else we wouldn't sign on."

"But nobody can count on luck, Elias," she said with a rueful smile. "Your ass-brained philosophy notwithstanding."

He took a deep breath, sensing what was to come. "Is this about settling down? Getting married?"

Her laugh reminded him of the serene fountain that burbled quietly in the arboretum's center. "I know you too well to ask you to do that, Elias. Besides, I didn't say I wanted to retire permanently. I just need a few years away from the job."

He frowned, suddenly worried that she was slipping away from him. Or vice versa. "A few years away. To do what?"

"I want to have a child," she said, taking his hand. "With you."

Vaughn was poleaxed. He nearly fell over.

Then he thought about it. A child. *Their* child. What an affirmation of life creating and raising a child would be. For the first time he could recall in decades, he felt tongue-tied.

"Let's talk," he said, even though he knew that words were no longer necessary.

Toscana, Earth
2355 Old Calendar

"How's my birthday girl?"

"Daddy!"

The late Commander T'Prynn's namesake launched herself at Vaughn's legs, grabbing hold with a strength that nearly sent both father and daughter sprawling across the lawn. The air was redolent with marigolds, zinnias, and fruit punch, the sounds of happy children aloft on a gentle breeze. Five candles burned on the cake on the backyard picnic table.

Little Prynn disengaged herself from Vaughn to chase Danilo, the neighbor boy. Ruriko approached Vaughn, greeting him with a wide smile, though she couldn't conceal her curiosity about his most recent assignment, out among the Orion crimelords. He smiled. There would be plenty of time to bring her up to date later.

Right now, whatever he could spare of himself belonged to little Prynn. Vaughn was delighted to see that he had beamed in soon enough to catch the bulk of the proceedings. Although the piñata was already spent and in pieces, candles remained to be blown out, yellow cake had yet to be served, and a goodly heap of ribbon-bedecked gifts remained tightly wrapped.

An urgent hail came in on Vaughn's combadge. He breathed a silent curse. *Why didn't I just ditch the thing?*

Ruriko noticed, scowling. But he knew she understood. He stepped away from the children to answer the call.

He braced himself to tell them that he couldn't interrupt little Prynn's special day.

But the call was from Admiral Presley's office. There was a coup brewing on the Elaysian homeworld.

But it's Prynn's special day.

The planet faced imminent political upheaval, a threat to the lives of tens of thousands of people, with the potential of spilling over into adjacent sectors. Countless people were in jeopardy.

Countless strangers. Prynn is my flesh and blood. And she needs me.

According to Admiral Presley, the mission couldn't wait. Starfleet's brass were counting on Vaughn's expertise. Once more unto the breach, dear friend. . . .

He glanced at Ruriko. How he envied her ability to simply walk away from it all. He watched Prynn, still chasing Danilo through the yard, the epicenter of a sudden squall of childish laughter.

Prynn. On her special day.

Duty. Indispensability. The lives of complete strangers.

He sighed and signaled that he'd be ready to beam out in five minutes. Long enough to explain, at least a little bit, about what he had to do. And where he had to be for the next few weeks.

Prynn will understand, he told himself. Just as Ruriko had understood half a decade earlier, when duty had placed parsecs between them on the very day little Prynn had come into the world.

U.S.S. T'Plana-Hath
2369 Old Calendar

Commander Vaughn sat alone in his quarters. Before him on the desk the images of Prynn and Ruriko smiled at him from a holocube. Ruriko's hair was streaked with gray now, but she'd lost none of her beauty, her smile had lost none of its wattage. And Prynn, now a grown woman, was definitely favoring her mother.

And she was wearing a Starfleet cadet's uniform. Today, Vaughn recalled, was to be her first day at Starfleet Academy. Searching his soul, Vaughn realized that he felt somewhat ambivalent about his daughter's career choice. Was she flattering him? Trying to emulate him? Or was he simply upset by yet another reminder that his inability to say no to Starfleet had made him an absentee father? Vaughn never had any doubt that Ruriko understood him, or had at least learned to love him in spite of whatever grave character flaw kept returning him to the field.

Vaughn reached out and touched the image of his daughter. How he longed to talk to her. To congratulate her for passing the Academy's stringent entrance exams. To offer her periodic encouragement and sympathy over the next four grueling years.

If only this mission didn't require subspace radio silence.

Ruriko, who had always been more than just the job, had been able to walk away from the field. Vaughn knew that he could not, at least not until death or senescence made the question moot.

He sincerely hoped that Prynn would take after her mother in that regard as well.

Uridi'si,
2369 Old Calendar

Vaughn stood on the bridge of the *U.S.S. T'Plana-Hath,* beside the captain's chair—the chair that his departed friend T'Prynn might have occupied by this point in her career, had she lived. On the viewer, Uridi'si's two suns had just risen above the planet's limb, painting the oceans every imaginable shade of green and blue.

Captain Sotak turned his chair toward the tactical officer. "Is the A.I. still contained within the planet's magnetosphere?"

The young woman at the tactical station displayed the no-nonsense attitude Vaughn had come to regard as typical of Vulcans who'd had little experience around humans. "The subspace jamming satellites are functioning normally, Captain. The *U.S.S. Valkyrie,* orbiting at antipodes, confirms this as well. The cyberentity cannot leave the planet's magnetic field lines. At least, not via subspace channels."

"Very good," Sotak said, swiveling his chair toward Vaughn. "Commander, this is your mission. How would you like to proceed?"

"We need to destroy the physical substrate the A.I. is using to run its computational cycles," Vaughn said. "Have your engineers found a way around the force field the thing has thrown up around itself?"

"Negative," Sotak said. "Not without compromising the safety of the several hundred people who are trapped inside the mining station dome."

Vaughn silently cursed the mining station's force fields, though he understood well the need for such strong defenses so close to the Cardassian border. Orion pirate raids were also a recurring problem in this sector.

But he also knew that the situation was far from hopeless. "Commander Tenmei has been working on an alternative way around the A.I.'s defenses, Captain."

The turbolift whooshed open at that moment, depositing Ruriko onto the bridge. She was back in uniform for the first time in two decades, now that Prynn had emptied the nest by enrolling at Starfleet Academy. Vaughn could see that the job and its accoutrements still fit her well. Except for the gray in her hair and the stiff-collar design of her uniform, it was as though the intervening years had never occurred.

Ruriko took her place beside Vaughn and the captain. "After all these years it's hard to believe that we've got to take down Cren Veruda's A.I. all over again."

"I still have to wonder why it's reconstituted itself only now," Vaughn said.

"I suspect we're dealing with a single rogue copy of the software matrix," Ruriko said, "which has been contained in an isolated system until very recently. Something must have changed that, and now it's growing again like kudzu. And since it's essentially an artificial life-form, it has an instinct for survival. It'll seize control of every computer it can reach if we let it."

Vaughn scowled. "When we didn't hear from the thing for thirty years after the first time we disabled it, I sort of assumed we'd seen the last of it."

"Obviously not," Sotak said.

Ruriko nodded. "An artificial intelligence capable of networking itself across the subspace bands is also capable of secreting copies of itself in unexpected places. Say, within the computer of a freighter on its way to the mining station down there."

It could spread itself across the universe like dandelion seeds on the wind, Vaughn thought. *If we're careless. Or unlucky.*

Vaughn noticed a look of surprise on the tactical officer's face, which she promptly hid behind a wall of Vulcan calm. "I'm detecting a significant fluctuation in the local subspace fields. The disturbance is localized less than fifty thousand kilometers from the planet."

Sotak's brows rose in curiosity. "On the screen, Lieutenant."

The blue-green world vanished from the viewer, replaced by an image of an irregularly shaped vessel which the tactical overlay revealed to be more than twice the length of the *T'Plana-Hath*. And it was heading toward the planet. A chill seized Vaughn's soul the moment he saw the alien ship. Beside him, Ruriko stifled a gasp.

"Analysis?" Sotak said.

The tactical officer appeared to be doing her best not to appear frustrated. "The vessel just emerged from some sort of transwarp fissure. But it corresponds to no known configuration."

"I've seen this type of ship before," Vaughn said.

Ruriko nodded gravely. "Me, too. It's Borg."

Maybe we don't have to be careless, Vaughn thought. *But we're already unlucky.*

Both the *T'Plana-Hath* and the *Valkyrie* were no match for weaponry of the small Borg vessel. Within minutes of engagement the *T'Plana-Hath* was crippled and the *Valkyrie* had fallen back several thousand kilometers.

Vaughn, Ruriko, and Sotak watched helplessly as the Borg vessel sent a shaft of blinding energy down into the Uridi'sine atmosphere.

"The Borg vessel is linking with the mining station. It appears to be conducting a transfer of data."

Vaughn realized then that the entire mission was a failure. "Veruda's brainchild must have somehow made contact with the Borg before we cut off its access to the subspace bands."

"Why would it wish to draw the attention of the Borg?" Sotak said, clearly puzzled. "The Borg would only seek to assimilate it."

"Or maybe," Vaughn said, "the A.I. thinks it's sophisticated enough to assimilate the Borg."

"Combining all it knows about Cardassian armaments with the Borg's most lethal technology," Ruriko said. "God only knows what a merger like that could do to the Federation."

"We may already be too late to prevent it," Sotak observed. "The Borg should be able to upload the A.I. in seconds."

Ruriko shook her head. "Ordinarily, yes. But the data feed is being attenuated by the mining station's forcefield. It's going to take a couple more minutes at least."

Vaughn looked into Ruriko's eyes. "Is the prototype ready?"

"*Ready* is a relative term. Remember, my command telemetry can be jammed the same way we're jamming the A.I. So I won't be able to control it remotely. I'll need to deploy the weapon on-site."

Vaughn swallowed hard. "Assemble your away team, Ruriko."

"Already done. Unfortunately, the transporter's out, so we'll have to rely on the *Valkyrie* for our beam-in. And we can't beam anywhere until we pierce the mining station's defenses."

The tactical officer was suddenly as close to beside herself as Vaughn had ever seen a Vulcan get. "The Borg vessel has ceased its data upload."

So the A.I. has copied itself onto the Borg vessel, Vaughn thought. *Very bad.*

"And it's powering up its weapons again!"

Sotak called for a red alert, but it quickly became clear that the *T'Plana-Hath* was not the Borg ship's target.

The mining station was. Before Vaughn's horrified eyes, a tremendous explosion flared up near the planet's equator. The A.I. down there was dead—along with hundreds of innocent people.

On the screen Vaughn could see that the Borg vessel was preparing to break orbit. *With a copy of Veruda's A.I. aboard. Now the damned thing can spread from here to the Delta Quadrant.*

There was time for only one decision. Vaughn knew the members of Ruriko's team intimately. They were good, but none of them had her combined expertise in A.I. and nanoscience. And only her mastery of both disciplines—as well as each team member's assistance—could ensure the correct deployment of the prototype.

Ruriko spoke up, evidently thinking that he was taking too long to decide what course to take. "We both knew it might come to this, Elias. Let's get on with it."

Vaughn nodded, feeling blasted inside. Unable to trust his emotions, he allowed his training to take over, as though he'd just placed a shuttlecraft on autopilot.

"Commander Tenmei, execute the plan. Take it directly to the Borg."

She didn't hesitate. She knew what had to be done, just as he did, as well as the cost. He watched as she opened a com channel at one of the vacant stations. "Disassembler team, prepare for immediate transport onto the Borg ship. *Valkyrie,* this is Commander Tenmei. Please beam our away team aboard and prepare to pursue that Borg vessel."

A *Valkyrie* bridge officer acknowledged Ruriko's request and asked when the team expected to need an evac.

She chuckled. "Tenmei out."

Ruriko faced Vaughn. "Goodbye, Elias. It's been a wonderful life at times."

Rare times. Those times between missions when I could get home.

"Goodbye," he whispered, his voice heavy with regret. The transporter took her.

Vaughn stood on the silent bridge, watching the images on the viewer. The *Valkyrie* slowly gained on the departing Borg vessel. After several tense moments the tactical officer confirmed that the away team had made it aboard.

Ruriko's static-laden voice scored the air, relayed by the *Valkyrie.* The weapon had been deployed. Trillions of tiny nanites, molecule-sized machines guided by Ruriko's short-range subspace pulses and keyed to find and unwrite the Veruda A.I.'s underlying code, were already coursing through the Borg ship's information conduits. She confirmed that the A.I. already seemed to be dying, apparently already too distracted to force the Borg to propogate its subroutines over the subspace bands.

But the team had to stay long enough to be sure.

If only this ship could maneuver, Vaughn thought, digging his fingers into his palms until they bled. *Maybe Sotak could buy enough time to evac the away team, once Ruriko's satisfied that they're done in there....*

Explosions began to rack the Borg vessel even as it opened up a transwarp conduit and vanished from normal space. *Valkyrie* stayed with it.

The other ship's name hung over Vaughn like an accusation. *Valkyrie,* he thought. *Chooser of the slain. How appropriate.*

No one moved or spoke as Vaughn studied the empty starfield where the Borg vessel had been. Starfleet would understand that Ruriko and her team had exchanged their own lives for countless others. They would see it as Ruriko did. As the families of the other away team members surely would. Vaughn struggled to reassure himself that he had chosen the lesser of two evils.

"You made the only choice you could, Elias," Dax said. "You must know that. And it sounds to me like Ruriko knew it, too."

Vaughn nodded, but said nothing.

"I don't think there's anyone on this crew who blames you for wanting to restore Commander Tenmei. Nobody deserves what happened to her. But you can't let yourself lose sight of the bigger picture."

"I can't let this opportunity go by, Dax," Vaughn said. "I'm being given a chance to save her. How can I not take it?"

"I'm not saying you shouldn't," Dax said. "We need to investigate that wreckage, see if we can determine what its mission was. We need to find that changeling on the surface and try to return her to her own people. And you need to address this situation with Prynn. All those things can be done while Julian continues to treat Ruriko."

Vaughn released a long breath through his nose. "You're right, of course." For a long time he said nothing more, and try as Dax might, she couldn't begin to guess his mind.

Finally he asked in a quiet voice, "It isn't easy being my first officer, is it?"

Taken aback by the question, Dax didn't know how to respond at first. "No," she admitted. "I'd have to say it isn't. But then, I didn't take the job because I expected it to be easy."

Vaughn nodded as if confirming something he'd long suspected. "You know, I never expected to be in a position like this. That I would face a moment when I would put my needs ahead of duty. All my life, in every situation I was thrust into, I always felt as if I knew what the right decision was, even when I didn't want to make it. Always. Whatever saved the most lives, that's what I chose. And I knew down to the last cell of my body, from the moment you brought me that padd in the mess hall, what the right decision was here. But this time, I made what I knew was the wrong decision. Because I couldn't bear the thought of failing her again."

"These are extraordinary circumstances that no one could have foreseen," Dax said. "The odds that she alone would survive the crash, much less be detected by the very ship you and Prynn are serving on, have to be astronomical. Beyond astronomical," she corrected, and suddenly realized something she'd never considered until now. "It's an impossible set of coincidences."

"No," Vaughn said. "It isn't. There's an explanation for all of this, and until now I've managed to avoid looking at it too closely. But it's high time I dealt with it." Vaughn rose to his feet and Dax stood with him. "Assemble an away team and send them down to the planet."

"Aye, sir." Dax turned to go, but Vaughn stopped her. "Ezri."

She turned to look at him.

"Thanks for being my first officer," he said. "And my friend."

14

Why is it that everything always goes to hell around here at the most inconvenient time?

The thought hung over Quark's head like a black cloud as he stalked through the habitat ring. After years of navigating political changeovers, wars, religious upheavals, treacherous business partners, the FCA, the Orion Syndicate, and even democratic reforms on Ferenginar, it astounded Quark that he could still run aground in the Great River, even when he was about to set course for deeper waters.

He and Ro were supposed to be making plans to leave the station for good, but ever since that shifty Trill had killed Shakaar—*I knew he couldn't be trusted*—she'd refused to speak to him, or reply to his messages. She seemed to have forgotten all about the fact that she was supposed to be putting her life on the station behind her. They both were.

The thought of going to Rom's old quarters didn't help his mood. Not just because his idiot brother and former employee was now Grand Nagus of the Ferengi Alliance, but also because its current occupant was proving to be an even bigger pain in the lobes than Rom had ever been.

At least she's paying her rent on time, Quark thought. Subletting the rooms to Treir had its financial benefits, to be sure, but he felt he was being consistently overcompensated in aggravation. Still, Treir was an Orion female, and that alone made her one of the bar's main attractions these days. *Her,* he thought grudgingly, *and her heavily muscled protégé, that Bajoran dabo boy, Hetik.*

Dabo boy. Quark repressed a shudder, as he did every time the two words came together in his mind, and steeled himself as he stopped in front of Treir's door. He pressed the touchpad mounted into the bulkhead and signaled admittance.

There was no answer, but Quark could hear giggling coming from inside the room.

"Treir, it's Quark," he said brusquely. "Let me in, I need to talk to you."

"Go away," came the reply.

"That's no way to speak to your employer."

"It's my night off," he heard her say. *"Besides, I've got company."*

"Come on, Treir. Five minutes. That's all I'm asking. This is important."

Even through the metal door Quark's sensitive ears heard the satisfying sound of a sigh of resignation. *"I'm sorry about this,"* he heard her tell her visitor.

Probably Hetik, Quark thought darkly. *If those two are sleeping together, I'll have to watch them even more closely than before.*

The door opened, and to Quark's abject shock, Morn walked out.

"What the hell are you doing here?" Quark demanded.

Morn favored him with a waggle of his meaty brow before he lumbered passed and headed off down the corridor. With his jaw hanging, Quark turned back to the doorway to demand an explanation from Treir, almost bumping into her. With one hand on the door frame and another perched on her curvacious hip, Treir stood in the threshold and glowered down at him from her two-meter height. "This had better be important."

All questions about Morn suddenly evaporated as Quark focused on Treir. She looked terrible. Clad in dull gray sweatpants, floppy sandals, and a baggy T-shirt that read KISS ME, I'M IRISH, Treir looked . . . *frumpy.* Her long, lusterless hair was tied back in a knot, except for a few ropy locks that hung carelessly in front of her face.

"Are you sick?" he asked.

Her eyes narrowed. "It's my night off," she said through her teeth.

"Look, I'm sorry, it's just—I've never seen you so . . . relaxed."

172

She leaned forward menacingly. "Look a little closer. Do I seem relaxed?"

Quark swallowed. "Now that you mention it, no. Actually, you look like someone who's spent too much time around Morn."

Treir rolled her eyes and went back into her quarters. "What do you want?"

Quark followed her inside. "I just need to talk to you for a few minutes."

Treir dropped onto a massive plush couch and crossed her feet atop the coffee table. "You already said that. What's on your mind?"

"Ro," Quark said.

Treir dropped her head back and stared at the ceiling. "Oh, please, not this."

"Would it kill you just to listen to me?"

"Why me?"

"Because I need some objectivity," Quark admitted angrily. "You've seen Laren and me interact more than anybody, and I need to talk to someone."

Treir sighed. "Get on with it," she said resignedly.

Quark sat on the edge of a chair facing the couch and leaned forward as he spoke. "You know I'm giving up the bar."

Trier nodded. "Yes, I know. You aren't the first male I've met who disappeared into the unknown when faced with a midlife crisis."

"It's *not* a midlife crisis!"

"Whatever. Why are we rehashing this?"

"What you don't know is that Ro's supposed to

come with me," Quark said. "She resigned her commission."

That got Treir's attention. She sat up. "Why?"

"For the same reason I'm leaving: the Federation."

"Really," Trier grunted. "Huh. That's a surprise."

"What's so surprising?" Quark said defensively.

"Don't get all indignant, Quark," Treir said. "I just meant that I got the impression Ro was starting to like it here. I'm just surprised she'd want to leave."

"That's just it!" Quark said. "I'm starting to wonder if she really does. We've been talking for weeks about how our lives would change if Bajor joined the Federation, and when the idea to leave and go into business together came up, I thought she was all for it. She even told Kira she was quitting. Then Shakaar gets himself killed, and suddenly she's more driven than ever. It's as if I've ceased to exist. I haven't been able to talk to her since the assassination."

"Quark, what did you expect?" Treir asked. "That she'd turn her back on her planet during what may be its worst crisis since the Occupation?"

Quark stared at the floor, feeling frustrated and unsure how to articulate it. "I expected her to be honest with me," he said.

Treir looked back at him in silence for a moment, then said, "Quark, *I'm* going to be honest with you. I don't pretend to understand what's going on between you two. On the surface you seem as preposterous a couple as I've ever encountered. But you're right, ever since we escaped from the Orion Syndicate, I've had the opportunity to watch you both, and I can see that you two have managed to pierce the absurdity of the mere idea and actually made a connection."

Quark was unsure whether to be flattered or insulted. "What's your point?"

"Do you love her?"

Quark became flustered. "I don't know. No. Yes. . . . Maybe."

Treir smiled. "Then let her be who she really is, *whatever* that turns out to be. That's love. Anything else is just a transaction."

Quark continued staring at the floor, shaking his head. "I have to be who I am, too," he said quietly.

"And who is that exactly?" Treir asked.

Quark looked up and met Treir's gaze. "You wanna know the truth? I'm not even sure I know anymore. Everything I do now, every choice I make, I keep making Laren part of the equation, whether I mean to or not. And now I wonder if the only way she and I will ever get together is if one of us becomes something we're not. Which would kill it between us, wouldn't it?" *Been living on this station too long,* he thought. *I'm starting to think like these people.*

"Have you ever stopped to consider," Treir asked softly, "that the person you think you're turning into is the one you've been all along, and just never realized it?"

Silence fell on the room, in the midst of which Quark wondered if he should fire Treir—or give her a raise. Then the silence was broken by a thud against the wall, coming from the corridor. It sounded as if a body had been thrown against it.

Treir was on her feet at once. "What the hell was that?"

"Probably a Klingon who had a few too many," Quark said dismissively. "I've seen it before. Let security deal with it."

Ignoring his advice, Treir went to the door and opened it. Quark chased after her. It wasn't a Klingon. A Cardassian was leaning heavily against the wall a few meters away. *And not just any Cardassian,* Quark realized. *It's Dukat's lookalike relative, Gul Macet. He doesn't look too good, either. Oh, frinx, please don't let it be another bad bottle of kanar. . . .*

"Are you all right?" Treir asked.

Macet was grimacing in pain, jerking his head violently as if experienceing some kind of attack. His hands clawed at his own face, drawing blood.

"Yuck," Quark said.

Macet opened his eyes, seeming to fight to focus them on Quark and Trier, his lips moving soundlessly. He started to fall, but Treir ran up to him and caught him before he hit the deck.

"Heeelllllpppp mmmeeeee . . ." the gul rasped.

Quark found a corridor companel. "Quark to infirmary. Medical emergency on the habitat ring. Section 015, level two. It's Gul Macet." If it was the *kanar,* at least he'd could say he tried to save the man's life. *What's that smell?*

"Goddess, what's happening to him?" Treir said.

Quark looked. Macet was staring up at Treir. The

gul was still trying to speak as a thin trail of smoke wound its way up from his open mouth.

Treir turned him over, probably thinking that Macet might need to vomit whatever it was that had gotten into him. *Never seen* kanar *do* that.

And there on the back of his neck, Quark saw something that looked like a pale blue thorn wriggling.

15

"It could be anything," Kira said, frowning at the energy profile displayed on the sciences station monitor on the bridge of the *Gryphon*. "I mean, it's obviously residue from the distortion field created by a cloaking device, but the telltale fluctuations that would identify it as Klingon, Romulan, or something else are completely absent."

The science officer, a Tellarite named Croth, agreed with her. "One might almost say it's *generic*," he said. "I realize that isn't terribly scientific, but it best describes what we're seeing here. This field shows no sign of any of the unique modifications that cloak-enabled species utilize to enhance the effectiveness of such technology. In that regard, it's very—what's the human expression?—'no frills.'"

"So it's either very sophisticated," Mello interpreted, standing behind Kira with her arms folded across her chest, "or very *un*sophisticated."

Croth smiled as he looked up at Mello, his eyes narrowing to tiny slits. "Aptly put, Captain, but there's no real way to know which based on the current data."

"I assume you've tried a tachyon sweep?" Kira asked. Over the years it had been learned that such sweeps could be most effective in exposing a cloaked ship. Usually.

Lieutenant Spillane, the security officer standing opposite Kira, nodded. "We've tried it hourly since before we left the Bajoran system. Nothing. Whatever's generating this field is constant. We can't even tell how far ahead of us it is, and we're already pushing warp 9.5."

"What's our ETA at Trill?" Kira asked.

"Twenty-nine hours," Montenegro answered.

"We hope to catch our quarry much sooner than that, Colonel," Mello said, trying to be reassuring.

Kira considered that. "What about Starfleet ships in Trill's immediate vicinity? Could they intercept—?"

"Admiral Akaar has already made arrangements for the three ships nearest Trill to sweep the region," said the captain. "And Starfleet forces stationed on the planet are on high alert."

"What if the Trill government tries to protect the assassin?"

No one answered. She suspected none of them wanted to consider that possibility. That was when Kira realized the larger implications Mello and her crew were facing. If Trill tried to protect Gard, it meant a Federation member government was complicit in Shakaar's assassination. And where would that lead? Revolution on Trill? Secession from the Federation? Trill being thrown out as a rogue nation? Schism as other worlds started taking sides? War? This was much bigger than Bajor, Kira realized. This had the potential to tear the Federation apart.

"Captain," someone called from across the bridge. It was Lieutenant Grigoryeva, the operations officer. "I'm detecting a spike in one of the EPS conduits in engineering. Looks like it's building to an overload."

"Can you cut power?"

"Not from here."

Mello went to her command chair. "Bridge to engineering."

"Bhatnagar here, Captain. We're aware of the problem. I'm trying to reduce— Neil, help me get this out of—"

The sound of an explosion filled the bridge.

"Engineering, what happened? Bhatnagar, this is the captain. Report!" Mello glanced at Montenegro, who didn't hesitate. He was on his way to the turbolift even as Mello was alerting sickbay. Kira found herself rushing to follow the first officer into the turbolift.

"Engineering," Montenegro said, then looked questioningly at Kira.

"Thought I might be able to help," Kira said.

The first officer nodded, but was obviously preoccupied with whatever had gone wrong in engineering, muttering, "I told her we were taxing our power systems."

Kira frowned. "Who? The engineer?"

Montenengro shook his head. "The captain."

Kira wondered what to make of that. Most first officers knew better than to publicly voice disagreements they might have with their C.O.s. *Montenegro looks pretty young, though,* Kira noted. *He can't have had this post too long. Maybe it's just inexperience.*

They traveled the rest of the way to engineering in silence. Two medics were already running down the corridors when they stepped out of the turbolift: one of them was Dr. Mei Ling Xiang, *Gryphon*'s chief medical officer. Kira had met her during the initial briefing after she'd beamed aboard from DS9.

The doors to engineering split open as they approached. Coughing crewmen poured out on a cloud of smoke, two of them supporting a man with some of the worst plasma burns Kira had ever seen. The crewman set the wounded engineer down on the deck and Xiang immediately went to work. "Conduit burst right next to him," one of the crewmen panted. "We were able to get to Hallerman easily, but the chief is still in there. She's pinned beneath a bulkhead. A couple of the techs were working to free her, but the room filled up so fast, the vents couldn't keep up."

"Status of the warp core?" Montenegro asked.

The crewman shook his head. "I'm not sure, sir."

Montenegro cursed and looked at Kira. "Ready?"

"Let's go," Kira said at once. Together they ran into engineering, unable to see more than two meters in front of them. It was hot, and the Klaxon was blaring. Montenegro felt for a locker near the door and retrieved two filter masks. He handed one to Kira, who finally allowed herself to breathe as she fit the device over her nose and mouth.

"I need to check the warp core!" Montenegro shouted over the alarm, his voice muffled through the mask. He pointed. "Bhatnagar is probably in that direction. Can you help them get her out?"

Kira nodded and started moving. Two steps later Montenegro was already invisible through the smoke, and her skin was slick with sweat. *Ventilation system must have been affected by the explosion. This room should be clear by now.*

Kira began to see shadows in the smoke. Two crewman in breathing masks were straining to lift a slab of debris off a woman who was pinned almost to her neck. As Kira drew close, she recognized the woman as another attendee of Mello's staff meeting: Lieutenant Commander Savitri Bhatnagar, chief engineer. Her burns didn't look as bad as Hallerman's.

One of the crewman noticed her. "She's out cold. I think she may have some broken bones," he said. "When we lift, you pull her clear."

Kira nodded and positoned herself behind Bhatnagar's head. The woman was coughing spasmodically. Kira took off her mask and put it over the engineer's face. Then she slipped her hands under Bhatnagar's shoulders and managed to get a grip under her armpits. "Ready!" Kira shouted over the Klaxon.

"On three," the crewman said. "One . . . two . . . *three!*" The crewman and his partner heaved. The slab lifted and Kira slid the engineer out. The crewmen dropped the slab with a crash, and one of them helped Kira lift Bhatnagar and carry her out of engineering.

As they set Bhatnagar down for the doctor to work on, Kira saw that the earlier patient, Hallerman, his rescuers, and the other medic were already gone, probably on their way to sickbay. Kira sat back and coughed, wiping her forehead with her sleeve. "Will she be all right?" she rasped.

Xiang didn't look up as she tended to her patient. "A few burns . . . a broken ankle . . . Most of the damage is to her lungs, but it's nothing I can't fix. Whoever put the mask on her saved her life. A few more seconds exposed to that stuff and her lungs would have been seared beyond repair." She looked at Kira, who was still coughing. "You should report to sickbay, Colonel."

"In a minute," Kira said, trying to breathe normally. "How's Hallerman?"

Xiang shot her a quick smile. "He'll make it, too."

Kira nodded and grimaced. Her chest felt as if it were on fire. She rose to her feet and tapped her combadge. "Kira to bridge."

"Mello here. Go ahead, Colonel."

"There were two injuries in the blast, Captain. Both are expected to make a full recovery."

"Good," Mello said. *"What about the warp core?"*

"Montenegro is checking on that now," Kira panted. *Where the hell was he?* "Stand by, Captain."

Just as she was about to reenter the engine room, *Gryphon*'s first officer staggered out, soaked with sweat and panting as he took off his breathing mask. Kira grabbed his shoulder to steady him as his hand reached for his combadge. "Montenegro to bridge. The warp core is stable. I've rerouted the plasma flow from the damaged conduit, but we still need a crew to work on venting the engineering section. All things considered, though, it could have been much worse."

"Good work, Commander. I was worried we might have to drop out of warp."

For a second Montenegro's eyes darted to Kira.

"Lieutenant Grigoryeva is coordinating the repair crews. Report to the bridge when you get cleaned up."

"Yes, sir. Montenegro out."

Two corpsman arrived with an antigrav gurney for Bhatnagar. While they tended to the patient, Xiang stepped up to Montenegro and Kira and scanned them with her medical tricorder. She scowled. "Both of you, get to sickbay now, before I call the captain and get her to issue the order. Thirty seconds of your time is all you'll need to give up."

Montenegro nodded wearily. "All right, Mei. We'll be there in a few minutes, I promise."

Xiang sighed and followed the gurney down the corridor, shaking her head.

Montenegro looked at Kira and rolled his eyes. "Doctors. Thanks for pitching in, by the way."

Kira tried to tell him she was glad she could help, but wound up making a noise that sounded more like she was clearing her throat.

Montenegro frowned. "Are you all right?"

Kira nodded and managed to say in a hoarse whisper, "Chest hurts. I think I'm inclined to follow the doctor's orders."

"Ouch," Montenegro said. "Yeah, you sound awful. Come on. I'll take you to sickbay."

True to Dr. Xiang's word, Kira's treatment took only half a minute to complete. When it was done, the pain in her chest was gone, and she was speaking and breathing normally again. Montenegro, on the other hand, insisted that he felt fine, that he'd kept his mask on the entire time he was in the engine room, and no amount of cajoling by the nurse would convince him to sit down and relax. Kira had seen this sort of behavior before—had been guilty of it herself, in fact: officers who thought it was important for every member of the crew to visit the doctor except themselves. In this particular case, though, Montenegro seemed preoccupied, and Kira got the distinct impression he had something to say to her, because he'd made a point of waiting during her treatment.

They exited together to the sound of Xiang's renewed threats to inform Captain Mello of Montenegro's apparently customary lack of cooperation with the medical staff, and it wasn't until they were inside a turbolift again that the commander did something that truly surprised Kira. "Halt," he instructed the lift. "Colonel, may I speak with you?"

"Of course, Commander," Kira said. "What's on your mind?"

"I realize we don't know each other very well, and I really shouldn't be discussing this at all. But I think it would be even less appropriate if I brought the matter up with another member of the crew, and I could really use the benefit of an outsider's perspective."

Kira frowned. "What is it?"

Montenegro sighed as if searching for the right words. "It's about Captain Mello." He waited to see Kira's reaction, perhaps thinking she might cut him off immediately for the breach of protocol. Discussing one's commanding officer with a third party was a touchy matter, but Kira didn't feel right shutting Montenegro down when this was clearly something he needed to unburden himself about. When she said nothing, he continued, "She's become . . . I guess the word I'm looking for is *distant* of late. I don't know how else to describe it. And it's not just the occasional bad mood. I'm talking about a change in personality."

That gave Kira pause. "Have you mentioned your concerns to the CMO?"

Montenegro shook his head. "Frankly, I've been afraid to. You may not know this, but I haven't been the ship's X.O. that long."

Kira smiled. "How old are you, Commander?"

Montenegro looked embarrassed. "Twenty-five, sir. I received a battlefield promotion during the war. My assignment to *Gryphon* came afterward."

He feels in over his head, Kira realized. *Like Nog, sometimes.* The war had turned a lot of junior Starfleet officers into seasoned combat veterans very quickly, and fatalities among more experienced officers had resulted in young men and women being thrust by necessity into jobs many of them weren't ready for. Becoming executive officer of an Akira-class starship at age twenty-five must have been overwhelming.

"I really don't know that I can tell you anything helpful, Commander," Kira said finally. "It isn't my place to advise you on your relationship with your commanding officer. I will say this: unless you feel Captain Mello's behavior is putting the ship or members of the crew in danger, any changes she may be experiencing are nobody's business but her own."

"Of course, you're right," Montenegro said. "And it's not that I think she's become a bad captain. It's just that . . . when I first came aboard, she took me under her wing. It seemed like we developed a rapport. Now I feel like I don't know her anymore."

Now, that I can relate to, Kira thought. "It's a difficult thing when a person close to you changes, personally or professionally," she said.

"You understand what I'm talking about," Montenegro said.

"I think I do, but unless you plan to bring it up to Captain Mello directly, this is something you'll have to work out yourself."

Montenegro nodded. "Resume," he told the lift.

They rode the rest of the way to Kira's deck in silence. She found herself unable to think about anything except Shakaar.

Later that ship's night, after Mello had commended Kira for her contribution in saving Lieutenant Commander Bhatnagar's life, and various members of the

crew had offered her their personal thanks, Kira retired
to her cabin and tried to sleep. It came to her slowly;
she was still wired from the day's events. But after she
finally dozed off, at the midpoint of *Gryphon's* voyage
and eighteen hours out of Deep Space 9, Kira was
awakened by a call from the bridge.

"Kira," she responded, forcing herself to alertness.
"Go ahead."

"Sorry to wake you, Colonel," the duty officer
said, *"but you have a priority message from Deep
Space 9. It's encrypted for your eyes only. Shall I
relay it to your quarters?"*

"Yes, thank you." Kira sat in front of the companel
and keyed the message. After the computer verified
her retinal scan and voiceprint, the screen resolved
into the face of Leonard James Akaar.

*"Colonel. I sincerely hope this has not reached
you too late. But because I no longer know who you
can trust, I felt compelled to send this as an encrypted recording, rather than try to speak with you
live. I fear that the situation is more dire than any of
us imagined. Listen carefully. We have verified that
First Minister Shakaar was under the influence of an
alien parasite, a member of a hostile and extremely
dangerous species known to both Starfleet and Trill.
This creature has been controlling Shakaar for
months, using him to advance its kind's hidden
agenda, which somehow involved Bajor's entry into
the Federation. It was for this reason that Shakaar
was murdered: to thwart whatever the parasites were
trying to achieve. I know this news comes as a shock,*

but I assure you the evidence we have is incontrovert-
ible. And more, we believe that another of these crea-
tures has infiltrated Gryphon.

"*Ro was right about the assassin. We have cap-*
tured Hiziki Gard here on Deep Space 9. There never
was a cloaking signature leading toward Trill. We
believe this was a ruse created by the creature
aboard the Gryphon *in order to reach Trill and use*
the ship to attack the planet in retaliation. You can-
not permit this, Colonel. The threat posed by this
species is not just to Bajor, but to worlds throughout
the Alpha Quadrant.

"*Unfortunately, there is no way for us to know who*
the parasite has taken over aboard Gryphon. *How-*
ever, there should be a classified security file in the
ship's computer, XENO-02884/1, that will tell you
everything Starfleet knows about these creatures. You
will need the following access code to decrypt the file:
Akaar Kappa One One Seven Override Twelve.

"*You must stop the* Gryphon *from reaching Trill,*
Colonel, no matter what the cost."

The recording ended, and for a moment Kira simply stared dumbstruck at the Federation emblem that
filled her companel screen. Then her hands began to
fly over the interface console, retrieving and decrypt-
ing Akaar's top-secret file: a classified report from
over a hundred years ago by one Fleet Captain
Christopher Pike, detailing a disastrous first contact
with a symbiont-like life-form inside a rogue comet.
Three more reports from only twelve years ago by
Captain Jean-Luc Picard, Dr. Beverly Crusher, and

Admiral Gregory Quinn, describing a horrific conspiracy that almost succeeded in taking over the United Federation of Planets.

Prophets . . .

She read the file a second time, her thoughts a maelstrom of denial and realization. Part of her simply couldn't believe the insidious nature of the threat they were facing: creatures that subsumed identities, attacking not only their hosts, but entire civilizations from inside. *And all that time I kept asking myself what was wrong with Shakaar, why he'd been acting so different, why he'd changed so much. . . . It wasn't really him at all, but some monster inside controlling him.* She found herself wondering whether any part of him had understood what had happened, if the real Shakaar had been trapped inside all that time, screaming to get out while that *thing* used his body, his voice, his position. . . .

Now another monster is walking the decks aboard Gryphon.

Montenegro's words came back to her: *"She's become . . . distant of late. . . . I'm talking about a change in personality."*

And about Shakaar's visit to the *Gryphon:* *"He spent most of his time with Captain Mello."*

Mello.

Captain Elaine Mello, who had herself suggested pursuing the alleged energy reading to Trill after reporting its discovery to Akaar. Mello, who had made such a passionate effort to lower Kira's guard when she came aboard. But those suspicions, Kira knew, weren't enough to go on. She needed more proof, and she suspected she knew where to find it. But she was going to need help.

Kira dumped Akaar's message and the file onto an isolinear chip and quickly dressed. Then she spoke. "Computer, locate Commander Montenegro."

16

When the door chimed, Prynn was ready for it. "Come," she said, knowing who it would be.

The door opened and Vaughn walked in, his expression grim. "You okay?"

She glared at him from her bunk. "You care?"

"Yes, as a matter of fact, I do," he said, his voice shaking.

Woah, Prynn thought. *His voice never shakes.*

Prynn sat up. "Dad, why are you doing this?" she asked. "Was that really Mom? It was her, wasn't it?"

Vaughn just stood there, watching her.

"Dad . . .?"

"You can stop now, Prynn."

"Stop what? Why won't you—"

"Enough!" Vaughn snapped, then continued in a

softer tone, "Enough. I just want to know one thing: How long have you been searching for her?"

"Searching?" Prynn said, her brow knotting. "Dad, I don't understand."

"How *long,* Prynn?"

She stared back at him blankly. "You can't think that I planned this? My God, I don't even believe we're having this conversation. Mom's alive and you're chasing conspiracies? *From me?* Why are you doing this? Why won't you let me see her?"

Vaughn's eyes narrowed. He shook his head, smiling as if at some private joke being replayed in his mind. "Oh, you're good," he said quietly. "You're very good. If it wasn't for the present situation, I could almost believe you're as innocent as you pretend."

Prynn felt her jaw trembling. "If you don't think I'm innocent, that must mean you're convinced I'm guilty of something."

"Not of anything that'll land you in the brig," Vaughn said. "But I thought—I hoped—we were beyond lying to each other."

That's when Prynn's anger rose up, overcoming her measured expression of hurt before she could get it back under control. It all happened in less than a second, but the smug, satisfied look of victory in her father's eyes confirmed that it didn't escape his notice. The pretense was over. She let the anger through, let her eyes become hard as she met his gaze. "Who the hell do you think you are?" she whispered.

"I have a better question, Prynn," Vaughn said. "Who are you?"

Prynn laughed. "Oh, you don't want the answer to that."

"Try me," Vaughn suggested.

She spread her hands. "I'm the daughter of Elias Vaughn," she said, as if it explained everything. "You want the truth? All right, fine. Yes, I've been searching for Mom since the day you came to the Academy and told me she was lost on a mission. You don't grow up as the only child of two Starfleet spooks without learning a thing or two. And for four years, ever since I graduated, I've found ways at every posting I accepted to search for Mom. That was *my* 'secret mission.' What did I have to lose? Every ship I was on, every sensor array I came in contact with, I modified it to search for her unique transponder signal. You aren't the only one who memorized it, Dad. I know yours, too. I admit it, I never really expected it to work. The odds were too remote. But I had to do *something*. She was my mother. Finding her in the Gamma Quadrant was beyond my wildest hopes, but I won't apologize for never giving up on her, even though you did."

Vaughn let the accusation slide. "You didn't do it alone, you know."

"What?"

"Finding your mother," Vaughn said. "You're right to think that the odds were remote. They were beyond remote. There was no way anyone could know what really happened to her, whether or not she survived, or where she'd end up if she did."

Prynn shrugged. "So I got lucky. I don't need to question it."

Vaughn sat down next to her on the bunk and looked at her intently. "Maybe you should. Think about it, Prynn. Your search for your mother succeeded only because of *Defiant*'s mission to explore the Gamma Quadrant. That mission happened only because I proposed it when I decided to transfer to Deep Space 9. And I made that decision only because of my encounter with that Bajoran Orb."

She stared at him. "You're trying to tell me that this all happened because of the wormhole aliens?"

"I really don't know," Vaughn told her honestly. "But I think something beyond my understanding, or yours, put me on this path I'm following. It's the path that made me change my life. The same path that led me back to you. The same path that led us, together, to this place, at this time. I know it sounds crazy. You know me, Prynn. I've never been a believer in much of anything. But look at everything that's happened. Against all probability and all reason, I have a chance to save your mother, to make up for what I did to her."

"It wasn't your fault, Dad," Prynn whispered. "When are you going to stop blaming yourself?"

He tilted his head. "You've been blaming me for seven years."

"I was wrong. I realized that when we encountered the Inamuri," Prynn said. "Dad, why are you doing this? What does it matter why this happened? You said it yourself, we can save Mom."

"It matters because my decision to try to save your mother is based on my belief that I'm meant to. I've been letting that belief override my duty to this ship, its crew, and the Federation. It makes me a bad captain, and that should scare the hell out of you."

"Well, it doesn't," Prynn said. "Look, I can't pretend I understand what happened to you in the Badlands, or that I can take seriously this idea that we're caught up in some 'destiny' you seem to think you're fulfilling. But if the last three months have taught me anything, it's that you're not a bad captain. You're not even a bad father, really."

"How can you say that?" Vaughn asked. "I was never there."

"But, Dad, that's just it—you were always there," Prynn said. She felt no anger now, no resentment. Just the need for her father to understand what he meant to her. "Whether we could be together or not, I never once doubted how much you loved us."

Hesitantly Vaughn reached out and put his arms around his daughter, pulling her close. "Oh, God," he whispered, unable to keep the laughter out of his voice. "You are so screwed up."

Holding her father tightly, Prynn echoed the laugh. "Chip off the old block, that's me."

They held each other in silence for several minutes and then Vaughn said, "Would you like to see her?"

She pulled away and looked up at him. "You'll let me?"

"If you really want to. But I have to warn you, she's in bad shape. Bashir thinks she's in a coma, and he still isn't sure he can bring her out of it, or even if there's anything left of her to revive."

"I don't care," Prynn said, rising to her feet. "I

want to be with her, Dad." She took his hand. "I want us both to be with her."

With some help from Bashir's artifical stimulation of her brain activity, Ruriko's human physiology had begun to reassert itself. Respiration, circulation, immune system, cell growth—all were beginning to respond favorably. Even her color had improved. She still hadn't awakened, but for the first time since this whole thing started, Bashir looked optimistic, albeit guardedly so.

Prynn stood close to Ruriko and wept silently as she stared into her mother's mutilated face. Still hairless and marred by scars and Borg implants, Ruriko continued to stand motionless in her alcove, one entirely cybernetic arm and shoulder already gone, along with several segments of body armor that had covered her earlier.

Then, very softly, Prynn started to hum. Gradually the humming became words, until she was singing a lullaby to her mother. Vaughn recognized the tune immediately: *Calaiah vel D'nai* by Rowatu, Ruriko's favorite, a song she listened to whenever she was sad. And as Prynn sang, Vaughn realized he'd never heard his daughter sing before, never known how beautiful her voice was, never realized how much it sounded like Ruriko's.

Suddenly the singing stopped, replaced by Prynn's sharp intake of breath. Vaughn was jolted out of his stupor and looked at her mother, scarcely daring to believe what he saw.

Ruriko's eyes had opened.

She was staring at Prynn. And more than that, her mouth was moving—fishlike motions that seemed meaningless. Vaughn called to Bashir, who came running. He looked stunned when he saw Ruriko, then turned to study medical monitors set up beside the alcove and nodded excitedly. "Keep it up, Prynn. Don't stop."

Tears streaming from her eyes, Prynn resumed her song. Ruriko continued staring at her, lips opening and closing, until, finally, she found her voice. It was barely a whisper, but it was unmistakable.

"Puh . . . puh . . . prrreeeeeeeeeeeen . . ."

17

Ten hours away from Trill, Dr. Xiang looked up and said, "I can't believe what you're suggesting."

The three of them—Kira, Montenegro, and Xiang—were gathered in the dining area of Montenegro's quarters. The doctor and the first officer were seated at the table, arguing back and forth. Kira paced the floor restlessly.

"I can't believe it, either," Montenegro agreed. "But it's true, Mei. It all fits. Admiral Akaar's message to Colonel Kira, the file she obtained from *Gryphon*'s own computers—what else do you need to convince you?"

"Proof!" Xiang said. "So far all I've heard is a lot of guesswork based on circumstantial evidence. What proof do you have that it's the captain?"

This is taking too damn long. Kira turned and slammed an isolinear chip down on the table.

Startled, the doctor's eyes darted to the chip, then back to Kira. "And what exactly is that?"

"The program that the parasite used to fake the cloaking-device reading. It was uploaded from the captain's quarters. Commander Montenegro found it after I told him about my suspicions."

The doctor looked at Montenengro.

"It's true," he said. "She created a fake datastream, uploaded it to the sensor arrays, and waited for the bridge crew to detect it. I took the report to her myself, and she contacted Admiral Akaar to suggest that *Gryphon* pursue it. She needed an excuse to head for Trill at high warp without revealing herself."

"But why? What's on Trill?"

"Revenge," Kira said. "These parasites, whatever they are, have some connection to Trill. It was a Trill who killed First Minister Shakaar, and Shakaar was the host to one of these life-forms. Akaar thinks the thing inside Mello could be using *Gryphon* to launch a retaliatory strike."

"This crew would never carry out an order to attack a Federation planet," Xiang insisted.

"They won't have to," Montenegro said. "Using the right codes, Mello can voice-authorize the main computer to fire phasers, empty the torpedo tubes, even eject the warp core toward the planet. She could kill millions of people."

The doctor looked trapped. "So what do you propose? A mutiny? How can you even think—"

"She's not your captain!" Kira hissed. "Not anymore! Didn't you listen to the admiral, or read Captain Picard's report? These parasites subsume the identities of their hosts and use them to achieve their ends."

"But I can't—"

Kira came around the table, grabbed Xiang's chair, and turned it roughly so that Kira was speaking directly into Xiang's face. "Look, Doctor. No one is suggesting we kill her. If she submits to arrest quietly so Commander Montenegro can assume command of *Gryphon* and return us to Deep Space 9, all this could end without bloodshed. But we need to be prepared to fight for control of the ship if we have to. One way or the other, though, I promise you, I'm not going to allow this ship to reach Trill."

Xiang stared into Kira's eyes for a long moment, then seemed to sag within herself. "What do you need from me?"

Montenegro breathed a sigh of relief. "We'll need you to try to save her, to separate the captain from the creature. It's not clear how long a parasite needs to be joined before separation becomes fatal to the host, but if there's a chance to cure Captain Mello, you're the one to do it. There's a physical symptom of the creature's presence in the host: a pale blue gill like a barb protruding from the back of the neck, just below the base of the skull. Once we confirm the presence of the creature, you'll need to keep her sedated. That file we gave you contains all the medical information Starfleet has on these creatures and their effect on humanoid bodies. While you're attempting to separate them, we'll inform the crew of what's happened."

Xiang took the chip out of the companel next to her and stared at it, shaking her head before she looked back at the ship's first officer. "I hope to God you're right about this, Alex."

"Then here," Kira said, tossing Xiang one of three phasers on the table. The doctor fumbled to catch it. Kira handed another to Montenegro and kept one for herself. "Let's get this over with."

"What should we expect?" Xiang whispered as they marched down to the captain's quarters. A quietly issued order from Montenegro had managed to clear the corridors nearest Mello's cabin, at least temporarily.

"Like it said in Dr. Crusher's report," Kira said. "Enhanced physical strength, along with extreme resistance to pain and injury. Phasers on stun won't work. If you have to fire, you need to set your weapon to kill."

Xiang halted. "You said we wouldn't need to—"

"I said we had to be prepared to fight for control of the ship," Kira said hotly. "That's what we're going to do."

"Colonel, please," Montenegro said gently. "Doctor, the evidence we have is that a phaser at that high intensity will only incapacitate a parasite host, not kill her."

"But you can't be certain."

"No," Montenegro conceded. "But we do know that a lower setting won't even slow it down."

Xiang gritted her teeth and upped the setting on her weapon.

They reached Mello's quarters. By consensus, Kira took point. She hit the doorchime.

"Come," came the reply.

The doors parted. Mello was seated on her couch, reading. "Colonel, this is unexp—"

Kira stepped inside and raised her phaser. "Get up," she ordered. "Slowly."

Mello's mouth dropped fractionally. Then she frowned. "If this is a joke, it's in the poorest possible taste."

"I said get up!" Kira snapped. "We know what you are, and what you're trying to do. But it's over. We can do this the easy way or the hard way, but I'm warning you, after what your kind did to Shakaar, I'm looking for an excuse to end your miserable existence."

Mello set down her book and rose slowly. "You're making a mistake."

"Hands over your head," said Kira. "Step to the middle of the room."

Mello complied.

"Xiang," Kira said. "Do it."

The doctor cautiously approached the captain, phaser ready. She stepped around Mello and lifted the captain's long brown curls, searching. Finally she said, "It's not here."

Kira went cold. "Look again."

Xiang did, and shook her head. "I'm telling you, she's clean. I . . . *Alex, what are you—?*"

Kira spun around, seeing Montenegro smiling at

her from the corridor an instant before the doors snapped closed.

Prophets, no!

She ran to the door. A force field knocked her back. *It was him all along—!*

There was the sound of someone hitting the deck behind her—

Kira spun around again, phaser up, and froze. Xiang was unconscious on the floor, and Mello was holding the doctor's phaser. She and Kira stood there at arm's length from each other, each one holding her weapon inches from the other's eye.

Montenegro smiled as he ran down the corridor, tapping his combadge. "Computer: initiate program Montenegro One, thirty-second delay."

There was a chime of acknowledgment. *"Program will initiate in thirty seconds,"* the computer said as Montenegro entered a turbolift.

"Bridge," he said. He was still smiling as the lift ascended.

18

With a profound feeling of déjà vu, Nog followed Bowers through the forest to the mock campsite they had set up before. They had beamed down at the site of the Borg wreckage with Gordimer, Shar, and T'rb. It was the task of the latter three to enter the ship and retrieve one of the Borg corpses. Commander Tenmei's neuroprocessor—the device every drone possessed that contained its specific instructions from the collective—had been destroyed when she was damaged. Shar and his team would need to beam up a dead drone and extract another neuroprocessor in order to find out the exact circumstances surrounding the *Valkyrie*'s mission to the Gamma Quadrant.

Bowers and Nog, meanwhile, had a decidedly different job: convincing the changeling to return with them.

"So, what do you think our chance of success is?" Nog asked Bowers. "Two percent? One?"

"I'm not worried about not succeeding," Bowers said, adjusting his tricorder. "I'm worried about what happens if we do. A Founder on the *Defiant,* that's something to keep the security staff up at night. I heard about the one who almost took control of the old *Defiant* before the war."

"It did take control," Nog corrected absently as he double-checked his own equipment. He hadn't been with Starfleet then, but he'd heard the story enough times from Chief O'Brien. "Captain Sisko almost had to destroy the ship."

"Great," said Bowers.

"But most of what it accomplished, it could do because people didn't know at first that it was there. Ezri says we're just going to return this one to the Dominion, since we're not at war anymore. I don't think it'll have any reason to try and harm us."

"Does it need a reason?"

Nog shrugged. "They don't think they're a lot like us, but I don't know. They do think about their actions. Not like the Borg." He and Bowers exchanged another look. Nog was pretty sure having a Borg drone on board would keep security up at night, too. It might keep *him* up.

"We'd better get a move on. Ready?"

"If that changeling is halfway across the planet by now, we're sunk."

"I don't think it is," said Bowers. "There's nothing

here to interest it. When we showed up it was just waiting in that wreck. It's ready to leave."

Probably since the day it got here, Nog thought.

"After two years it's got to know the Dominion doesn't know it's here," Bowers went on. "We're its only way out. It may be scared, but it may also want to find us again even more than we want to find it."

The nonessential equipment they had left behind did not appear to have been disturbed, and Nog packed it up regretfully. He hoped Bowers was right about the Founder sticking around, but he was afraid Bowers was wrong.

They were headed farther north when Bowers gestured frantically for quiet and Nog froze, then glanced down at his tricorder. Just on the edge of their sensor range was the Dominion ship. And inside, again, were the faint humanoid readings they had picked up when the first arrived.

Bowers had doubled back to where Nog stood and now hissed in his ear, "We're going in, and this time, *no noise!*"

Nog nodded to show he understood.

They approached the ship from the south, under the engine pylon. Although Nog was now familiar with the interior of the ship, the act of returning felt even more surreal. The smell of decay and moss still pervaded the air, and Nog tried not to wrinkle his nose. His feet sloshed as he moved toward the source of the humanoid readings: the bridge. Try as he might, he had a difficult time picturing the Founder sitting calmly within the wreckage, surrounded by attending corpses.

Then he turned the corner and she was there, waiting, sitting on her haunches in a puddle of brackish water. She looked up at them, calmly, her face blank of expression. "I thought you left," she said, in a voice that sounded as young as she looked. She seemed completely unaffected by the Jem'Hadar skeletons less than four meters away.

"No, we didn't leave," Bowers said. "We returned to our ship. But our vessel is still in orbit."

Her face didn't change. "Why?"

"We wanted to find you," Nog said, finding his voice. She turned her attention to him but didn't say anything. "To apologize," he improvised. "We didn't mean to hurt you before." Ezri had been less than thrilled to discover they had hit the Founder with a phaser blast.

She regarded him carefully. "It didn't hurt," she said. "It surprised me. I didn't know you could do that."

"Yes," he said. "Another Founder showed us how to do it."

At that the girl did react—she looked angry. "No Founder would show you how to do that," she said. "You're lying."

Bowers was shooting him a warning glare, *Don't make her mad,* but Nog had figured from the beginning that the only way to close the deal was to put Odo on the table. "Maybe not a Founder who grew up with you," he said shrewdly. "But what about one of the Hundred who were sent out to

208

live among solids? That's who our friend Odo was."

Now she looked suspicious as well as angry. "I know about Odo," she said. "He rejected the link. He caused the death of another Founder. He was cast out."

"No," corrected Nog. "He went back to the link, after the Federation and the Dominion made peace."

"There is no peace between the Federation and the Dominion," she said.

"There is," Bowers interrupted. "We even have a Jem'Hadar living among us in the Alpha Quadrant. He was sent to us by Odo."

She considered this. "I understand that kind of peace," she said. "You have Vorta, also, overseeing you, and many Jem'Hadar."

"No—" Bowers started to say, but Nog quickly interrupted.

"I don't understand what a Jem'Hadar is doing there myself, actually. If you come back with us, I'm sure Taran'atar will tell you all about it. You could even order him to accompany you home," he added, ignoring Bowers's incredulous stare. *I win, everybody wins.* Looked at in the right light, it was even, finally, putting one over on Constable Odo.

"Taran'atar. This is your First?" she asked.

"He's First aboard our station," Nog said.

"My First is dead," the Founder said, and pointed at a body across the bridge. Her look turned almost melancholy. "I miss First." *Incredible to think anyone could actually miss a Jem'Hadar.* At various points throughout the mission, Nog had found he missed everyone he knew on board the station—with one exception.

"I'm, uh, sorry for your loss," Bowers said into the sudden silence.

"I miss Second, I miss Fourth . . ." As though aware of how that sounded, she stopped. "I do not miss Third," she said decisively.

"Good riddance," Nog agreed under his breath. Bowers elbowed him in the ribs.

"Do you have a name?" Bowers asked the girl.

"What use would I have for a name?" she replied. "I am but a drop in the ocean."

"Aren't we all?" Bowers muttered.

"Why did you come back?" the Founder asked.

"We came to invite you up to our ship. When we leave, we can take you with us."

"To your quadrant."

"For a short while, yes," Bowers said. "From our station, we'll send a message to the Dominion, let them know we found you. You'll be able to go home. That is, if you want to."

"Your station . . . where you have your Jem'Hadar."

"Absolutely," said Nog, who could see her waving goodbye from the platform already, Taran'atar packed and at her side. He tried to look so sincere that it hurt.

She regarded him carefully for a moment, then turned back to Bowers. "I was taught to believe that solids can never be trusted." Before Bowers could respond, she added, "But I trusted my own kind to come for me, and here I have been these two years. I'm ready to leave this place. I accept your offer."

* * *

Vaughn marched into science lab one and looked into the faces of the officers awaiting him. Their guest, the young changeling, was studying the corpse of a Borg drone stretched out on a lab table. "Report," he said.

"Sir," Shar began, "we've decrypted the data encoded into the neuroprocessor and have been able to verify the *Valkyrie*'s mission to the Gamma Quadrant. Apparently since its assimilation seven years ago, the ship and its crew have been used by the Borg for reconnaissance, as a prelude to larger-scale incursions by the Borg if new species are detected and determined to be desirable for assimilation.

"Three years ago, during the Borg's most recent incursion into Federation space, the Borg ship that attacked Earth apparently updated its Federation database from the ships it destroyed and transmitted that knowledge to the collective. Two items in particular that caught the collective's attention were *the Dominion* and *changelings*. The Borg spent the next year erecting a transwarp conduit that would open into the Gamma Quadrant, and eventually deployed the *Valkyrie* as their advanced scout for the express purpose of finding a changeling and attempting its assimilation for the continued 'perfection' of the collective. The encounter with the Jem'Hadar ship two years ago was the result, in which both ships were destroyed."

"Do we know if the collective ever learned what happened to the *Valkyrie?*" Vaughn asked.

"We can't be certain," Bowers said. "But we know the Jem'Hadar managed to do considerable damage to the *Valkyrie* very early in the battle. As far as we can tell, the drones aboard were cut off from the collective almost immediately. It's very possible that the Borg decided they weren't prepared to deal with that much resistance. Or it may be that circumstances forced them to deprioritize the Gamma Quadrant—according to the Pathfinder database, the *Valkyrie*'s mission to the Gamma Quadrant coincided with the Borg first contact with Species 8472."

Vaughn nodded thoughtfully, recalling that the extradimensional alien civilization the Borg had encountered had very nearly destroyed the collective, and might have become an even worse scourge than the Borg had it not been for intervention of the *U.S.S. Voyager.* Small wonder that the Dominion became a lower priority to them. "Excellent work, gentlemen. We need to make this data available to the Dominion as well as Starfleet Command."

"The Dominion, sir?" Bowers asked.

"Think about it, Sam," Vaughn said. "Preparing the Dominion for the possible return of the Borg can only help us in the long run, and I can think of no better way to demonstrate our own peaceful intentions than by returning a marooned Founder to their keeping, along with the information you've obtained. This isn't just a tactical opportunity, it's a diplomatic one."

"I hope Command agrees with you, sir."

Vaughn smiled. "That makes two of us."

A scream suddenly cut through the lab. Vaughn turned and almost refused to believe what he saw.

The Borg corpse had come to life. Assimilation

212

tubules had launched themselves from its inanimate hands and into the nearby changeling, whose form was morphing wildly before his eyes.

Bowers drew his phaser, ready to fire.

"No," Vaughn shouted. "Not yet."

The child's terrifying howls continued. Black streams of nanoprobes snaked through the Founder's undulating mass of metaplasm. Pseudopods reached out blindly across the room as it convulsed in apparent agony, lashing out in every direction. The *Defiant* officers narrowly missed being struck by a pseudopod that smashed into the bulkhead behind them.

Then all at once the morphing mass contracted, straining violently to compress itself into a tight opaque sphere. It vibrated madly on the deck as it continued to shrink, becoming Borg-black as it condensed.

"Prepare to fire," Vaughn said.

Suddenly the sphere morphed again, expanding and elongating into the changeling's humanoid form. She seemed to be struggling to maintain her shape before finally stablizing.

Shar took out his tricorder and began scanning.

"Are you all right?" Vaughn asked.

The changeling nodded, flexing her hands.

"You resisted the assimilation," Bowers said. "How?"

A third arm grew out of the center of the Founder's narrow chest and opened its slender, symmetrical, two-thumbed hand. The arm lengthened until the hand was only inches away from Bowers's face. In

213

the center of its palm, Vaughn saw, was what looked like a black pebble.

"The nanoprobes?" Bowers guessed.

"They were trying to overwhelm me," she said. "They were quite painful. They kept twisting me inside out. I knew I had to make them stop. So I did the only thing I could think of. I squeezed them together until they stopped."

"Mr. ch'Thane," Vaughn said. "Explain, please."

Shar shook his head. "She's fine. She really was able to withstand the assimilation."

"How?" Bowers asked.

Shar continued studying his tricorder. "Borg nanoprobes are designed to assimilate life-forms on a cellular level. But a changeling's morphogenic matrix has no cellular structure in its natural state. In essence, it was as if the nanoprobes were trying to assimilate a body of water."

"More good news for the Dominion, I guess," Bowers said. "And for us."

"Wait a minute," Vaughn said, peering at the Borg corpse across the room. "That drone is dead. How is it possible that the assimilation tubules are still functional?"

"The Borg are proving to be increasingly difficult to understand," Shar said, "but apparently, even without a living humanoid to act as host for the technology, the Borg imperative to assimilate other life-forms can survive the death of a drone under certain circumstances, lying dormant until the right opportunity presents itself."

"My God," Bowers said, looking at Vaughn. "That means—"

"Prynn," Vaughn said, drawing his phaser as he ran from the science lab. The medical bay was just down the corridor. . . .

Vaughn's phaser was up and aimed as he stormed into the room. But all was peaceful. Prynn was exactly as he left her, still at Ruriko's side, softly reading to her mother from *The Silmarillion,* Ruriko's favorite book. Ruriko herself seemed peaceful, even serene, her eyes almost tender as they regarded Prynn, never leaving her.

Tears began to form in Vaughn's eyes. *My family,* he thought, unsure who he was addressing. *This is my family. Isn't this why I'm here?*

Vaughn lowered his phaser. "Prynn," he said.

His daughter paused from her reading and looked up. She saw the phaser in his hand and frowned. "Dad? What's wrong?"

"I'm not sure," Vaughn said. "But I need you to step away from your mother right now. We have to make sure everything's all right. Please, Prynn. Move now."

To her credit, Prynn didn't argue. She put the book down and started to rise.

The tenderness abruptly fell from Ruriko's eyes. She reached out to Prynn with her remaining hand.

Vaughn brought up his phaser and fired.

19

Lieutenant Commander Bhatnagar had returned to duty only two hours before. After a good night's rest following her release from sickbay, she was anxious to figure out the cause of the overloaded EPS conduit. While by definition, starship engine rooms should have been predictable, uneventful places that operated according to the reliable mathematics of warp physics, she'd come to believe that, more often than not, they were in fact the nexi of entropy. Order battled chaos in these places with an almost dependable regularity. And engineers, she secretly suspected, functioned as avatars of both these forces, keeping them carefully balanced so that neither overwhelmed the other. Thus, warp drive worked, but the best engineers could still find a new wrinkle in the laws of physics when circumstances required it.

Bhatnagar stood over the master systems display table in the center of room and knew that something wasn't right. Nothing in the diagnostics explained the buildup that led to the plasma overload. According to every instrument and situation monitor in engineering, everything had been fine. Yet something had caused the conduit to rupture, and in the absence of any evidence of a malfunction, or defects in the conduit itself, Bhatnagar knew only one other conclusion was reasonable: sabotage. Someone aboard the *Gryphon* had caused the explosion deliberately.

She was considering how precisely to tell the captain when a chime from the computer suddenly rang out. *"Warning: Antimatter containment failing. Ejection system off-line. Warp core will breach in two minutes."*

What—?

Bhatnagar checked her monitors as all around her techs scrambled to do the same at stations throughout engineering. But nothing was amiss: Forcefields and injection systems in the warp core were at optimum, the core temparature was well inside the safe zone, and there was no indication of any anomalous energy fluctuations. Yet the computer had just announced imminent failure of the antimatter-containment fields.

"Montenegro to crew," the first officer's voice said over the comm system. *"Report to the escape pods. All hands abandon ship. I repeat, abandon ship."*

Bhatnagar was beginning to believe chaos had finally gotten the upper hand. Nothing was making sense. A breach in progress where all was well, and now an order to evacuate the ship.

"Commander! What the hell are you doing? Let's go!"

Bhatnagar ignored her assistant, Lieutenant Benitez, as she sought the cause of the computer's warning.

"Warning. Antimatter containment now at 50 percent and dropping. Warp core breach in sixty seconds."

"Savitri, we have to get out of here, now!"

"This doesn't make sense," Bhatnagar muttered, moving toward the towering column of the warp core itself. It pulsed normally, tranquilly. The ejection system really was off line, but . . .

Suddenly Benitez's hand was around her wrist, yanking her away from the core. "Commander, we've been given the order to evacuate. We have to go!"

Bhatnagar allowed herself to be pulled away from the core, still unable to believe what was happening as she started to run to the escape pod.

Mello's thumb tensed above the trigger. Her eyes never leaving Kira's, she tapped her combadge. "Mello to bridge." No response. "Bridge, this is the captain. Respond."

"Captain," Kira said, "you have to listen to me—"

"Shut up," Mello said, backing toward her desk. Without changing her aim, she activated the companel. "Mello to bridge."

"They can't hear you, Captain," Kira said. "Montenegro's put your quarters under security quarantine. That means a forcefield over the door, signal jamming, and, I suspect, neutralized phasers."

Mello tested her phaser on the door. Nothing happened. "Dammit," she said, tossing the useless weapon aside. Xiang still lay unconscious on the floor. "All right, Colonel. Start explaining to me what the hell is going on."

"Admiral Akaar sent me a message," Kira began, and with exacting detail, proceeded to explain the truth about Shakaar and his assassination. "Montenegro must have anticipated that he was in danger of being exposed, because almost from the moment I came aboard, he tried to convince me that something wasn't quite right with *you*. How you'd begun to distance yourself, how your personality had changed—all things that I'd seen in Shakaar the last few months. He even had evidence ready for us to discover that you were the one who'd faked the cloaking-device reading. He set me up, Captain, to get us both out of the way so he could take over the ship and carry out an attack against Trill."

Mello had begun pacing the room. "I attended a classified Starfleet briefing on this parasitic species just after I was promoted to captain, eleven years ago. There was compelling evidence to suggest they might someday return, but I never imagined—" She stopped, cut off by a Klaxon and the computer's announcement of a core breach in progress.

Kira tested the doorway. The force field was still there. Mello failed again to contact other parts of the ship. "Quarantine field should have come down automatically once the evacuation order was issued."

"Maybe it would have," Kira said, "if this were a real crisis."

"You think Montenegro engineered this?"

"I'm beginning to," Kira said. "That unexplained crisis in engineering gave him the perfect opportunity to set something up. Think about it. He can't just take command of the ship without an explanation the crew will accept. Confining you here, even killing you, doesn't help him. He needs control. But if he gets rid of the crew—"

"He's leveling the playing field," Mello realized.

Kira nodded. "The ship can proceed to Trill on autopilot, then all he needs to do is implement an attack program, or voice-authorize manual firing of the weapons systems. It's what he convinced us you'd be able to do."

"*Warning,*" the computer said. "*Antimatter containment now at 13 percent. Warp-core breach in fifteen seconds.*"

"If you're wrong, we're dead," Mello said. The decks vibrated beneath them. Outside the windows, escaping pods could be seen fleeing the ship.

Kira said nothing as the final seconds dwindled . . . and then passed. The *Gryphon* continued toward Trill at Warp 9.5 silent as a tomb.

Xiang awoke and took the news of what had happened better than Kira expected. Maybe it was because now at least there was no question about who the immediate threat was. Mello studied the chip with Akaar's message and the parasite file, which Xiang still carried, while Kira and the doctor searched for a way to break out of the captain's quarters.

Less than four hours from Trill, the forcefield in front of the door fritzed out. The women took positions in different parts of the room, ready to hit Montenegro from three directions. But the doors didn't open at once. The panels barely budged before several sets of fingers forced their way into the crack, pulling the doors apart.

Faces started to appear between the doors. Spillane. Bhatnagar. Croth. A half-dozen other officers and crewman Kira didn't recognize. "Captain," Spillane said. "Are you all right?"

"Nothing that kicking my first officer's ass wouldn't cure," Mello said. "Why didn't you evacuate with the others?"

"Blame Commander Bhatnagar," one of the engineers said. "She convinced us the ship wasn't about to blow up—the warp core was at optimum."

"Spillane and I both had similar suspicions," Croth said. "We were on the bridge when Montenegro came up unexpectedly, just in time for the computer to announce the alert so he could order the evacuation. We were already inside our pod when we started to question the situation. Thirty seconds to core breach, it occurred to us to ask the computer to locate you, but internal sensors suddenly went off-line. That's when we were sure that something weird was going on."

"When the ship didn't explode," Spillane continued,

"we tried getting back to the bridge, but it was sealed off. We started searching the ship section by section for anyone else left aboard, and that's when we ran into Bhatnagar and her team. They said their tricorders detected biosigns coming from your quarters."

"Good work, all of you," Mello said.

"Sir," Bhatnagar said. "Why is Commander Montenegro doing this? What is he after?"

"Colonel Kira and Dr. Xiang will explain on the way," the captain said.

"On the way where?" Spillane asked.

"The armory, then the bridge," Mello said, stepping out the door. "I'm taking back my ship."

Turbolifts were off-line. They had to take Jefferies tubes from deck to deck, using wrist lights because illumination abruptly cut out through most of the ship while they were raiding the armory. Using phaser rifles, cutting their way into the bridge once they reached deck one was relatively easy. And to Kira's surprise, nothing hazardous greeted their arrival. The bridge was dark and empty. Dim emergency lights cast stark shadows across the room, making the lights from the crew stations seem all the more intense.

Spillane went to the operations console and studied the ship's status. "We're still on course from Trill," she reported. "Speed is constant at Warp 9.5, and flight control is locked off."

"Computer," Mello said at once. "Take the warp engines off line. Authorization Mello-Pi-Four-Six-Two."

"Unable to comply. Emergency manual override in effect. Warp-engine control only possible from main engineering."

"Computer, locate Commander Montenegro."

"Unable to comply. Internal sensors off-line."

Mello cursed herself for forgetting. "Can we send out a distress call?" she asked Croth.

The science officer made a guttural noise of frustration. "Communications are off-line or disabled, I can't tell which."

Bhatnagar and her engineers quickly ascertained the extent of the damage Montenegro had done. Clearly realizing that he was still facing opposition aboard the ship, the first officer had abandoned the bridge while Mello and her team were preparing their assault. Evidently he hadn't had enough time to assume complete control of the ship, so he had concentrated instead on locking out tactical, communications, propulsion, and flight control from the bridge, routing them to engineering. He'd also sabotaged the control systems for transporters, turbolifts, and the internal security systems, which meant there would be no easy way of tracking Montenegro's movements, or using the life support system against him.

"The computer still recognizes my command codes, though," Mello said.

Spillane nodded. "That's the irony. He didn't even bother trying to override your codes. He just manipulated our systems enough to gain manual control of the areas he was interested in and disabled the rest."

"Like a parasite," Kira said. "He's using the ship like a host body, leeching what's useful to him."

"We managed to rescind all of Montenegro's access codes," Bhatnagar said, "but it may be too late for that to do us any good."

"What about autodestruct?" Mello asked.

Bhatnagar and Spillane exchanged looks. "You still have it," the security officer said. "You can activate it unilaterally now. But the time delay is disabled. Once you give the word, there'll be no going back."

"We may not have a choice," Mello said. "So he's in engineering."

"That's our best guess," Croth said.

"I'm going after him," Kira said, checking the charge on her rifle.

"Not alone, you're not," Mello said, picking up her own weapon.

"Captain, your place is on the bridge," Kira reminded her.

"Ordinarily, I might agree, Colonel. But until my people can fix the damage the parasite has done, I'm useless up here. One thing I *can* do is help you track down the creature and stop it. I owe Alex that much." Placing a backup hand phaser on her hip, Mello took two tricorders from the engineers and handed one to Kira. "With internal sensors off-line, we'll need to use these to find him. "Lieutenant Spillane."

"Sir?"

"You have the bridge. The colonel and I are going hunting."

"Where do you want to begin?" Kira asked.

Standing in the main Jefferies tube junction on the port side of *Starship Gryphon,* Mello held out her tricorder and slowly panned the room, scanning the six horizontal tubes that surrounded them, as well as the shafts above and below. "I found his combadge signal. It's coming from starboard and down, close to the navigational deflector."

"It's a ruse," Kira said. "He dumped his combadge there so we'd waste time going after it."

Mello nodded. "I agree. But I'm not picking up anything else that would suggest where he is."

"Engineering is the only place that makes sense," Kira said.

"Maybe," Mello said.

Kira tested the hatch for the tube that offered the quickest route to engineering. Locked. She searched for an access panel and pried it open. "I think I can override the seal, but it'll take a minute."

"Do it," said Mello.

Kira went to work. A moment into it, she said "Captain, I want to apologize to you for what happened in your quarters."

"That's all right, Colonel," Mello said, then added darkly, "Maybe someday I'll find some way to surprise you on Deep Space 9."

"I really made a mess of things. I led a mutiny against you, all because I let Montenegro manipulate me into thinking you were the most likely suspect to be the parasite host."

"But I *was* the most likely suspect," Mello pointed out. "Between what happened on Deep Space 9, the message you got from Akaar, and the lies Montenegro had been feeding you, you made the logical choice, and did what you thought was necessary to save lives. I'm not sure I would have acted differently if our positions had been reversed, given the circumstances."

"I was ready to kill you back there. I almost did."

"We almost killed each other," Mello corrected. "But isn't that the point, Nerys? This thing inside Montenegro tried to pit us against each other, to divide and conquer. It failed then, and it's going to fail now because were refusing to be divided." Mello suddenly shook her head and chuckled.

"What's so funny?"

"I have a confession to make, Colonel," Mello said. "When I first found out you were put in charge of Deep Space 9, I had my doubts about you. I didn't think it was right that a Federation starbase or its Starfleet personnel should be placed under the command of a non-Starfleet officer, allied or not, and I resented you even more when you were put in command of the Europa Nova evacuation. I think I would have felt the same even if I'd already known that your Starfleet commission was still active. Because the bottom line was, you didn't wear the uniform, and your loyalties were still to Bajor first. You were too provincial for my comfort, despite what your advocates in Command thought about you.

"But then I saw you in action during the Europani evac, and I knew that I was the one who was too provincial. I allowed myself to believe that because you didn't come up through the Academy, any leadership qualities you possessed, any of the experiences or abilities that brought you to where you are, had to be less than those of a Starfleet captain. I realize now those beliefs were unworthy of you, and unworthy of me."

Kira shrugged as she continued working on the lock. "Captain, I really don't understand what the point of all this is."

Mello grabbed her by the arm, forcing Kira to look at her. "Just this: Starfleet would be damn lucky if you decided to put on its uniform again. But if you don't, if the worst happens and Bajor and the Federation go their separate ways, then I think the loss to both sides will be incalculable. If I've learned nothing else during the last four months, it's that together we add up to something far greater than we'll ever be apart."

Kira made no reply, but she held Mello's gaze for a moment before returning her attention to the lock. "Think I've got it," she said. "Get ready. On three. One . . . two . . . three." The Jefferies tube portal opened to darkness.

Mello was checking her tricorder.

"Anything?" Kira asked.

"I'm not sure," Mello said. "I think he may have set up a jamming field."

"Great," Kira said. "Let me go first. You can continue scanning as you follow."

"Colonel—"

"Captain, I know this is your ship, and I know you feel you have a personal stake in taking the lead here, but you have to let me take point now," Kira insisted. "I've spent my entire life fighting in dark tunnels."

Mello hesitated, but even feeling the way she did at that moment, she had to know Kira was the best choice to go first. "Very well, Colonel. Lead on."

They began to crawl. Ten minutes into the tube, Mello reported she was picking up a life-sign dead ahead. And something else. An energy signature. *"Colonel, get down!"* Mello shouted.

Phaser fire lit up the Jefferies tube, narrowly missing Kira. She hit the deck, hoping Mello had done the same. The orange beams continued to flash over her head in the darkness, the sound of the discharges reverberating through the tube like thunder.

Suddenly the phaser fire stopped. Kira heard the distant sound of a hatch unsealing and immediately returned fire, hoping to tag their foe before he escaped. The echo of the hatch slamming shut testified to her failure. *"Dammit!"*

There was a soft moan behind her and Kira went cold.

Turning her body around, her wristlight found Mello, a blackened hole smoldering in the middle of the captain's chest. She was still conscious, staring back at Kira blankly, as if surprised.

"Kira to bridge! Captain Mello's been hit! Beam her directly to the bridge!"

228

"Transporters are still down!" the reply came.

"Then send down Dr. Xiang," Kira barked. "We're in port Jefferies tube 14A. Move it!"

"Belay that, Spillane," Mello said. Her breath came in short labored gasps. "You'll only expose Xiang to danger. Besides . . . even if Mei gets through . . . I'll be dead by the time she arrives."

"You're not giving up, Captain!" Kira snapped. "Xiang, get down here now!"

"No . . ." Mello insisted.

"Stop talking," Kira told her. "Save your strength—"

"Bridge," Mello pressed on, "I need you to bear witness . . . to what I'm about to do. . . . Stand by. . . ."

"We're standing by, Captain," Spillane said quietly, as if she knew what was about to follow.

"Computer," Mello began. "This is Captain Elaine Mello . . . commanding officer, *U.S.S. Gryphon*. . . . Transfer all command codes . . . to Commander Kira Nerys—"

"Captain, no—" Kira protested.

"Authorization . . . Mello . . . Beta . . . Seven-two-nine . . . execute."

"Transfer executed," the computer confirmed. "U.S.S. Gryphon *now under command of Commander Kira Nerys."*

"Elaine . . ." Kira whispered.

Mello groped for her Starfleet combadge. She pulled it off her uniform and placed it in Kira's hand. "Stop him, Nerys," she said through teeth clenched against the agony in her chest. "And take care of my ship."

Kira's eyes dropped to Mello's combadge. The silver arrowhead felt strangely heavy in her hand. She looked up again, but Mello's eyes were already blank and lifeless.

Kira sat in silence for a moment on the floor of the Jefferies tube. Finally she reached out and closed Mello's eyelids, slipped the captain's hand phaser into her boot, then placed the Starfleet combadge over her left breast.

"Kira to bridge."

"Yes, Col— yes, Commander?"

"Captain Mello is dead. I'm resuming pursuit of Montenegro." Checking the charge on her phaser rifle, Kira continued down the Jefferies tube.

20

Judith had to hand it to Miles—he'd figured out exactly which buttons to push to draw Dad out of his isolation. She knew he wasn't past his grief, but to see him in his kitchen again—once more conducting his unique symphony of pots and pans, food and fire—Judith was filled with hope for the first time since Ben had disappeared.

Dad had made jambalaya—a Sisko Family specialty—and from the first forkful, the O'Briens looked as if they'd died and gone to heaven. Of course, Dad always put too much cayenne pepper in his jambalaya, but Judith wasn't about to start that old debate now. Seated around the table, they talked about life in San Francisco. Keiko was working with a team of botanists at a civilian agricultural lab, where they were innovating new varieties of fast-growing food crops for those planets hit hardest during the war. It was rewarding work, she said, but she missed not being able to see her innovations put into practice.

Miles spoke at length about teaching starship engineering to Academy freshmen, how much more sane it was than spending his days and nights trying to keep Deep Space 9 from coming apart, or trying to stay ahead of battle damage aboard his old ship, the *Defiant*. Keiko leaned over and told Judith *sotto voce* that for all his protests to the contrary, Miles secretly enjoyed the chaos of the old days. Judith laughed, which made Miles wonder self-consciously what the two women were whispering about.

She noted that Dad seemed to take a sadistic joy in teasing poor Chief O'Brien—"You call yourself an engineer? You can barely boil water!"—and Miles played the role of the bumbling, replicator-dependent Starfleet engineer to the tee. He had correctly realized that Dad needed someone to blow off steam at, something he could never do in the same way with Judith or Kasidy, or even his loyal staff. But Miles was another matter. By lumbering his way into Dad's life, he'd given her father something to get mad about that he could fix.

And then there were the kids, who were having precisely the effect Kasidy had hoped they would. They filled the house with laughter again. And though they must have reminded Dad about the children he'd lost, Kasidy and Judith's hope had been that they would also make him think hard about the child still to come. Dad entertained them with yet another in a long list of tall—and contradictory—tales about the fake alligator suspended from the restaurant ceiling. The kids just ate it up.

"So what do you do in San Francisco, Molly?" Dad asked. "Lotta playing outdoors with your friends, I'll bet. Riding your bike down those amazing hills?"

"I don't know how to ride a bike."

"Excuse me?" Dad said.

"I don't know how to ride a bike," Molly repeated.

Dad looked up at Molly's parents in complete incomprehension.

Keiko looked embarrassed. "You have to understand, she grew up on a space station. . . ."

Dad rolled his eyes and shook his head, then turned back to Molly. "Well, I have a solution to that. I have an old bicycle in my basement that my son used to ride when he was your age. How would you like to have it?"

Molly's eyes lit up. She turned to her mother. "Can I, Mommy?"

Keiko grinned. "I don't see how we can refuse," she said.

"Yes!"

"That's just fine," Dad said, beaming. "You and your parents can try it out in the park, tomorrow. After a good night's sleep and a good breakfast."

"Sir, we wouldn't dream of imposing any more than we already have," O'Brien protested.

Dad's smile fell. "So what are you saying, Chief?

Are you going to deprive an old man of the company of these children?"

"No, sir. I just meant—"

"Never mind, never mind," Dad said, brushing off O'Brien's explanation. "I'm not taking no for an answer. You'll all stay the night, at least, and we'll have a fine time. And tomorrow, Molly can try her new bicycle."

"What do you say, Molly?" Keiko prompted.

"Thank you, Mr. Sisko," Molly said.

Dad laughed. *He laughed!* "You're very welcome, Molly. Of course, you'll need to take off that pretty necklace first. We wouldn't want anything to happen to such a lovely thing."

Molly touched the ornate silver chains around her neck, adorned with pendants of different sizes and shapes. Judith had noticed it when she first laid eyes on the girl. It wasn't like anything she had ever seen before, and she had to agree, it was lovely.

"May I ask where she got it?" Judith said to Keiko. "It's very unusual. Is it Vulcan . . . ?"

Keiko looked at O'Brien, who decided to answer the question himself. "Actually, it's Bajoran," he said quietly.

Dad's eyes darkened, but only a little. "Well, on your Molly it's positively beautiful, Chief," he said, then looked at him sternly. "She obviously takes after her mother."

Miles snorted and shook his head, sipping from his beer.

"Dad, enough already," Judith chastised him.

"Oh, I'm just kidding," Dad said, and slapped O'Brien on the shoulder, causing Miles to choke on his beer. "Anyone with children like these is welcome in my home any time. As long as he stays out of my kitchen."

"Noted, sir," O'Brien gasped, coughing. After a moment he went on, "You know, the necklace was actually a gift from someone. I don't think about it much anymore, because it happened the first year we were on the station, but it's actually a bit of a mystery."

"What do you mean?" Judith asked. "You don't know who gave it to her?"

"No, I do," O'Brien said. "It was Kai Opaka. She was the religious leader of Bajor at the time. The thing is, she was lost in the Gamma Quadrant right after that. See, she'd come to the station after spending her entire life planetside, and had asked Captain—I mean, Commander Sisko, to take her through the wormhole. I prepped the ship they took for the journey. Opaka and I passed each other in the airlock, and she was wearing that necklace. Then suddenly she looks at me—and I swear it was like she could see inside me—and she says, 'You have a daughter, don't you?' Now, I want to stress I'd never met this woman before. There was no reason for her to know anything about me, and Molly was only a year old at the time. But when I told her I did have a daughter, she took off the necklace and put it in my hand, asking me to give it to Molly. Then she stepped into the ship like she never expected to come back."

"So what happened?" Judith asked.

"She died," Miles confirmed, then added, "sort of. She wound up trapped on the surface of a moon in the Gamma Quadrant. There was nanotechnology—artifical microbes—in the biosphere that resuscitated anyone who died there, and Opaka had been killed when the ship crashed. She came back to life, but she was now dependent on the nanotechnology, which wouldn't function outside the moon's biosphere."

"So she was trapped there?" Judith asked, apalled.

O'Brien nodded. "I'm afraid so. I know Julian— Dr. Bashir, DS9's chief medical officer—worked for years on a cure, but he never had any success. Then we met the Dominion, and our dealings with the Gamma Quadrant became more complicated."

"Why would anyone introduce technology like that to an uninhabited moon?" Dad asked.

"Well, it wasn't entirely uninhabited," O'Brien said. "It was actually a penal colony for two small warring factions of a Gamma Quadrant species. They had refused to stop fighting, so they were sentenced to fight, and die, and fight again, forever. From what Julian told me, Opaka believed that what happened to her was preordained. She dedicated her life to teaching the factions peace."

"My God," Dad muttered, shaking his head.

"She sounds like a remarkable woman," Judith said.

O'Brien nodded. "I talked to Major Kira about it afterward. Opaka had been a force for peace and unity on Bajor for a long time. Her loss was a blow to everyone. But the thing is, she never doubted for a second that everything that happened to her was happening for a reason. She really believed she was serving a higher purpose, something bigger than herself."

Judith saw that Dad was listening attentively. The point of O'Brien's story clearly hadn't escaped him. "I understand what your trying to say, Chief," he said, shaking his head, "but my son—"

"Sir, with all due respect," O'Brien said, "I knew your son as a father, a soldier, a diplomat, a shipwright, an explorer, a religious icon, a baseball fan, not to mention an exceptional cook." This drew a smile from Dad, and Miles went on, "None of those things were responsible for what happened to him. From what I know, he sacrificed himself for a world he'd come to love more than himself. During his life he was responsible for saving countless lives. You should be proud of him."

"And my grandson?" Dad asked bitterly. "For what was he sacrificed?"

"Dad," Judith said. "I know you don't want to hear this, but you need to remember that Jake was a grown man. He was already taking responsibility for his life before the war ended. Wherever he is, whatever happened to him, he chose it."

"How can I know that, Judith? How can anyone know?"

"I don't pretend to know anything," Judith said gently. "None of us do. But are you so determined to assume the worst that you're afraid to have any hope at all?"

"Judith—"

"And what about Kasidy? While you're here missing Ben and Jake, she's missing them on Bajor, about to give birth to your grandchild. Doesn't that mean anything to you?"

Dad looked at Molly, humming contentedly to herself as she finished the last of her jambalaya. His gaze went to Kirayoshi, who a half-hour ago had demanded to be held and subsequently fell asleep in his mother's embrace.

With a sudden movement of his arms, Dad pushed his chair away from the table and stood. "I need to get up early. Judith, you'll see to our guests, won't you?"

Judith sighed. "Yes, Dad."

"Then good night," he said, and headed off to bed.

"That's it, Molly—keep pedaling!"

Keiko knew there was little chance of Molly falling over, as her father was holding the back of the antique bicycle that she was struggling to learn to ride. She even kidded him that everyone must have ridden bicycles when he was a little boy growing up on Earth, but he assured her that he wasn't *that* old. "I learned a lot younger than you when I was a little boy in Dublin," he said. "My brothers taught me. There's no better way to learn balance." He did admit that he'd skinned his knees more often than he made it from one end of the street to the other without falling off. But there was little risk of that happening to her, as he was holding on tight.

At least, that's what she believed until she looked over her shoulder and saw that her father was no longer holding on, and was still standing next to her mother at the far end of the block.

"Aaah!" Molly screamed as the front wheel lurched to the left, then right; before she knew what had happened, she saw the wheels of the bicycle swoop over her head and could feel the back of her elbow scraping on the rough concrete.

"Molly!" Miles O'Brien and his wife Keiko shouted in unison as they ran to where their child had fallen. "Are you all right?" said Miles, bending down to lift her up.

"Wow!" laughed Molly with a broad smile. "That was great!"

"I'll get a dermal regenerator," said Keiko, brushing off the back of Molly's pants as Molly stood her bicycle back up and started to climb onboard again. Before she could check Molly's arm, the little girl was off running down the sidewalk.

"Scrape already forgotten," said Miles, smiling as he watched his daughter wobble erratically off, fall, get up, laugh, and start over again. "She's a natural."

"She could never do this on DS9—or the *Enterprise,* for that matter," said Keiko. "Can you imagine Captain Picard's reaction to a child on a bicycle in the corridors?"

"Picard? What about Odo? I can hear him now: 'No pedaling on—'"

"'—my Promenade!'" thay finished in unison, Keiko dropping her voice down a couple of octaves. They laughed. "He always tried so hard to come across so stern, when you know deep down he probably wanted to turn into a bicycle just to find out what the fascination was."

"How's the bike working out?"

The O'Briens turned to see Joseph Sisko walking toward them.

"It's been wonderful, sir," Keiko said. "Molly's having the time of her life. We want to thank you again for your generosity, and your hospitality."

Joseph waved away Keiko's gratitude. "You don't have to thank me, Keiko. This visit has helped me to realize there's a lot more I need to be thinking about right now than my own feelings. In fact, that was actually what I came out here to discuss with you. I have a request to make."

Miles looked at Keiko, then back to Joseph, smiling. "Well, of course, sir. Anything."

Joseph grinned wryly. "I think you may regret saying that when you hear me out," he said. "I want you to take me to Bajor."

21

Dax sat with Prynn in the ensign's quarters, letting her vent the grief, the outrage, the anger, and the hatred she felt for Vaughn. He had tried to talk with her, Dax knew, but the shock of what happened was still too recent and too raw.

"He couldn't have been sure," Prynn was saying. "He says she was going to assimilate me, but how could he really know? Dr. Bashir said the autopsy was inconclusive."

Dax nodded. "I know. But he insists on what he saw, Prynn. And this was right after the Borg corpse down the hall tried to assimilate the Founder. Do you really think he was imagining it?"

Prynn covered her eyes with one hand, trying to rein in her emotions. "I don't know what to think. I just know we were so close . . . and he deliberately killed her. My father killed my mother. Again."

"You'll get no argument from him on that," Dax said. "He really believes that's true, that he's killed Ruriko twice. He may be more devastated by this than you are. But there's something you both need to understand and accept before this goes any farther: Ruriko Tenmei died a long time ago, as a hero, saving lives. The thing that was in sickbay wasn't her."

"What are you saying?"

"What I'm telling you is that Dr. Bashir's latest tests have confirmed what he feared all along: the damage to your mother's brain was too extensive. There was nothing left of her to bring back. She was all Borg."

"That isn't true. I saw her, I heard her. She responded to me. She said my name."

"Did it?" Dax asked, deliberately dropping the female pronoun. "It's hard to know exactly what it actually said, isn't it? I mean *really* know beyond any doubt. And the drone never said anything else, did it?"

"Why did she respond to me, then?"

"Julian believes it was a form of imprinting," Dax explained. "You were the first life-form the drone encountered when it regained consciousness. It targeted you for assimilation. But as weak as it was, with so many of its implants removed or neutralized, it need time to re-create its assimilation system. Do you understand what I'm saying? You weren't that thing's daughter. You were its target."

"I don't believe this."

"Dr. Bashir will confirm it if you ask him. It's up to

you. But if you believe nothing else I tell you, Prynn, I hope you'll believe this, as someone who once, in an earlier lifetime, allowed her spouse to die and remained estranged from her daughter for eight years because of it: neither you nor your father will recover from this unless you do it together. You need to decide if the grief and anger and hate you feel right now, and the self-loathing Vaughn feels, are stronger than the love I know you share."

Prynn shook her head, "I don't know if I can do this, Ezri."

"Prynn," Dax said softly. "It was the Borg that killed your mother. Don't let them destroy what's left of your family. Don't let them win."

Prynn said nothing, and after a moment Dax stood up and departed, promising to look in on her later.

As Dax expected, Vaughn was waiting for her in the corridor, a confused expression on his face.

Dax pressed an index finger to her lips and gestured for him to follow her. She led him up to deck one, and suggested they go to his quarters. Inside he asked the question that she knew he needed to ask.

"Why did you lie to her? There are no new test results. Ruriko *was* alive in there, somewhere, despite what the Borg implants were making her do. That much Julian was certain of before the end. He told me himself. She really was regaining her humanity, even if it wasn't strong enough yet to fight off the assimilation imperative."

"That's right, I lied," Dax said. "Someday you can

tell her the truth, Elias. Maybe when she's found someone who means to her what Ruriko meant to you. But until then, she won't understand that you didn't really kill Ruriko to save Prynn, or even to save the *Defiant*. You did it for Ruriko. So that whatever *was* left of her wouldn't have to live one instant with the horror of turning her own child into a monster."

Vaughn closed his eyes, and when he opened them again, Dax saw that they were rimmed red. "I think I finally understand what L.J. was trying to tell me before I left the station."

"L.J.?" Dax asked. "You mean Admiral Akaar."

Vaughn nodded. "He warned me not to take Prynn on this mission. He said he wasn't worried about the crew; he was worried about the two of us."

"There's something to be said about taking the advice of your elders," Ezri said lightly, knowing she didn't need to remind him that Dax's life spanned over three hundred years.

Vaughn laughed bitterly. "I might have guessed you'd still have some pearls of wisdom to dispense."

Dax shook her head. "Not really. Just a little common sense. Give her time. Give yourself time. And try to forgive yourself."

After Dax left, Vaughn sat on the edge of his bunk and stared at the deck for long minutes. His tears fell silently.

22

"Kira to bridge," she whispered. "I'm about to enter engineering. Stand by." Leading with her phaser rifle, Kira hit the control for the Jefferies tube seal, and the doors split, opening into light.

She heard no sound save the thrum of the warp core some distance away. Peering out, she saw that the tube opened into another junction room, with other tube entrances surrounding her, except for the single door that led out.

Taking a deep breath, she moved toward the door. It opened at her approach, and she turned into the next room quickly, searching for a target.

She had to creep through a few more sections before she finally spotted Montenegro in the warp-core chamber, bent over the master systems display table, his back to her. Knowing an easier shot would never come, Kira took aim with her rifle. Montenegro didn't turn, but she sensed a change in his attitude that made her certain he was aware of her. He was already a blur of motion as her finger pulled back on the trigger. The beam missed him, and he was gone from sight. Kira cursed and doubled back in the hopes of cutting him off from another direction.

"*Well, well,*" Montenegro said, his disembodied voice cutting through the vast engine room. "*So the gullible little Bajoran has made it all the way to the end of the maze. I almost wish I had some cheese to reward you with. You know, I think that's the thing we like most about your people, Colonel. As meat goes, you're so very easy to steer.*"

Kira spun as she crept around a corner, searching for the source of the voice. *Keep him talking.* "Is that what we are to you? Meat?"

Laughter. "*What else? You're lower life-forms, Colonel. Get used to the idea. You think walking upright, developing language, building starships, and fighting wars is a sign of superior intelligence? You have no idea what true intelligence is capable of.*"

"So tell me," Kira said, firing off a shot at a shadow that disappeared too quickly. The phaser blast blew a hole in the wall where the shadow had been.

Laughter again. "*Careful, Colonel, you might shoot something important. Not that I'm surprised. Humanoids think too much with their glands, and not enough with their brains. That's why you're all so easy to conquer.*"

"My people have been conquered before," Kira said, climbing up a ladder to the upper level. "It didn't last. I seriously doubt you'll do any better."

"The Cardassians? Please, Colonel. That only underscores my point. A more useless species of humanoids we've yet to encounter. But you Bajorans—you're the biggest joke of all. There you are at the threshold of time, space, and omniscience, and you squat on your mudball waiting for something to come through to you, rather than step inside yourselves. That's just one of many things we plan to correct."

The Celestial Temple? The parasites couldn't possibly pose a threat to the Prophets. Could they? "With such big plans, seems like you're wasting a lot of effort going after Trill." Kira peered over the balcony for some sign of Montenegro on the lower level. Nothing.

"You still don't get it, Colonel. You think the symbionts of Trill are benign little creatures sharing their intellectual immortality with the meat species on their planet. But believe me, they're even more dangerous to your kind than we are."

"How?" Kira asked, her eyes tracing the path she'd taken to the ladder.

She felt a breath in her ear. . . .

"Boo," Montenegro said.

Kira reacted instantly and swung the butt of her rifle with all her might against Montenegro's ribs. She felt a crunch, but *Gryphon*'s first officer didn't even flinch. Instead, he grabbed her by the neck and lifted her off the balcony with one hand, tore the

247

phaser rifle away with the other, and threw her over the railing.

Ingoring the choking pain in her windpipe, Kira tried to control her fall, landing hard but rolling in time to avoid a bone-breaking impact. She looked up.

With inhuman strength, Montenegro swung the phaser rifle against the balcony railing and the weapon shattered. Fragments showered her. Montenegro held on to the jagged remains of the rifle and leaped down effortlessly, landing on both feet in front of her. He showed her the pointed shard of metal he held and smiled.

Kira charged at Montenegro and started flailing him with her fists, each blow a direct hit to his face as she pummeled him repeatedly, left, right, left, and left again. Montenegro staggered back, making no move to deflect the blows, his head snapping back with each punch. At one point Kira felt bone cracking, but wasn't sure if it was her opponent's cheek or her hand. Feeling the strength in her arms starting to ebb, Kira pivoted on one leg and landed a devastating kick into Montenegro's chest with the other, knocking him back against a bulkhead.

Kira bent, hands on knees, panting as she waited for her enemy to fall to the deck. Instead, Montenegro stood up straight, flexed his neck, and said, "My turn."

Faster than she would have thought possible, he jumped up and spin-kicked her against the warp core. Her back hit the guard rail hard, and for a moment she found it difficult to breathe. Montenegro strode toward her without haste and kicked her legs out from under her. She was flat on her back when he suddenly reached down and grabbed a fistful of her hair, pulling her up to one knee. He forced her to look up at him, once again waving the shard of her phaser rifle above her.

Defeated, Kira's hands fell to her sides.

"Now, I want you to tell me something, Colonel," Montenegro said.

Kira's fingers found her boot.

"Now that you have some small indication here at the end of your stupid, brainless little life about what you're facing, do you really think *any* Bajoran has even the slightest chance against my kind?"

Her hand found Captain Mello's hand phaser.

"Why don't you ask Shakaar?" Kira whispered as she brought up the weapon and fired.

Montenegro caught the beam point-blank in the face. His head pitched back, followed by his body. His tensing hand yanked out a clump of her hair as he fell back, landing in a heap on the deck in front of the warp core.

Kira climbed to her feet and walked around the body, wanting to be certain he was dead. The beam should have taken his head off, but it didn't, though most of Montenegro's hair had been singed away.

Then his jaw moved.

Kira staggered back, expecting him to get up and attack her again at any second. Instead, something came out of Montenegro's mouth.

Led by a pair of oversize pincers, a clawed, six-legged creature small enough to fit in Kira's hand slowly emerged on a trail of blood. Its pincers felt the air searchingly before it suddenly scurried toward Kira.

Kira waited until the thing was half a meter away, then raised her foot and brought her heel down with enough force for the impact to echo through the engine room, sending a jolt of pain up her leg. She scarcely noticed, and proceeded to scrape off the smashed remains of the parasite against the lip of the warp-core base.

Kira then went to the master systems display and attempted to power down the engines. She tried once. Twice. Three times.

"Kira to bridge. Montenegro is dead, but whatever he's done to the engines, I can't stop it. Warp power is unchanged."

"We see it, Commander," Spillane said. *"Can you return helm control to the bridge?"*

"Stand by," Kira said. She searched the maze of Montenegro's reconfigured engineering console and found the manual override for helm and navigation. It was a search of only a few seconds to find the cancelation command. "Computer, this is Commander Kira. Transfer flight control to the bridge."

"Transfer executed."

"That did it, Commander! We can change course— oh, no . . ."

"What is it?" Kira demanded, an instant before the ship shook beneath her.

"Three Federation starships on attack vectors,"

Spillane said. *"They're ordering us to lower shields and power down, or be destroyed."*

Akaar, Kira thought. *Those have to be the ships that Mello mentioned. He probably ordered the attack if* Gryphon *got beyond a certain point without contact.* Kira searched the board once more, cursed, and started out of engineering. "Take evasive action. I'm coming up."

"Sir, communications—"

"Are not an option," Kira said as she searched the corridor for the turbolift. "He slagged both the subspace and RF transmitters. We're mute. We'll have to figure something else out. Bridge," she told the elevator.

Kira stepped onto the bridge to find the *Gryphon* officers glued to their seats. Spillane noted her arrival and stood up from the command chair. Without thinking about it, Kira settled into the center seat. The *Gryphon* shook again.

"They're targeting our after shields," Spillane reported.

"Show me a tactical display," Kira ordered.

A strategic overlay suddenly superimposed the starfield on the viewscreen. Their attackers were the Nebula-class *T'Kumbra,* along with the *Sagittarius* and the *Polaris,* both Norway-class starships. From the look of things, the two Norways were in pursuit, closing in from behind and below. Up ahead and above them, *T'Kumbra* was swooping down to intercept. They'd make very short work of the *Gryphon,* unless Kira tried to fight it out. But as far as she was

251

concerned, firing on another Federation starship was *not* an option.

"*T'Kumbra* . . ." Kira murmured, thinking.

"Incoming fire!" Spillane announced. "Hang on!"

Kira grabbed the armrests of the captain's chair as the ship rocked again.

"Shields reduced to forty percent," Bhatnagar said. "Sir, what are your orders?"

"Captain Solok still commands the *T'Kumbra,* doesn't he?" Kira asked the room urgently.

It was Xiang who answered. "I believe so, yes."

Solok, Kira thought. Abrasive, arrogant Academy classmate of Captain Sisko. Solok was so certain of the innate superiority of Vulcans over humans and most other Alpha Quadrant humanoids that he'd once challenged Benjamin to a game of baseball during a quiet moment in the middle of the Dominion war. Kira had played on Sisko's team, and they had lost spectacularly, but nevertheless claimed a victory by simply taking joy in playing the game—something the Vulcans would never do.

"*You are attempting to manufacture a triumph where none exists,*" Solok had said.

Kira smiled. *All right, Solok, let's see if you remember. . . .*

"We need to communicate with the *T'Kumbra,*" Kira said.

"But, sir," said Croth. "You said yourself that the transmitters were destroyed. . . ."

"We need to send Captain Solok a message," Kira insisted, "something he'll know immediately is from me so he'll order the task force to stand down. I need an alternative to conventional communications."

Croth considered. "We could tap out a message using the running lights on the hull," he suggested.

"No good," Kira said. "It might take them too long to notice, assuming they noticed at all. We need to get Solok's attention *immediately.*" An idea occurred to her. "What if we used the phasers?"

"Sir," Spillane said, "if we start using the phasers now, the task force almost certainly won't hesitate to use deadly force against us."

The ship rocked again. Bhatnagar reported shields were down to fifteen percent.

"I don't think they've been pulling their punches up to now, Lieutenant. Reconfigure the aft phasers to one one-hundredth power and fire short bursts away from those ships. We want to tap out a message in Starfleet's most basic code."

Spillane nodded, working her console. "I can do that, but it better be damn short, sir."

"Just two words: *Manufactured triumph.*"

The other officers looked at each other. Kira realized she must have sounded as if she were out of her mind. Fortunately, they all knew they had no time to argue with her.

"Firing phasers," Spillane said. Her hand danced rhythmically on her control interface. On the viewscreen the phaser beams flashed in perfect synch with Spillane's taps, firing harmlessly into the void.

Another blast shook the bridge. "Shields are gone," Bhatnagar announced, and Kira knew she had failed.

"Sir," Croth said suddenly. *"T'Kumbra* is matching course and velocities alongside us. *Sagittarius* and *Polaris* are doing likewise above and below."

Kira rose from her chair and stared at the viewscreen, now showing an image of the Nebula-class ship. "Any new transmissions?" Kira asked.

Croth studied his console and shook his head. "Negative. However, their torpedo tubes are open and loaded."

Kira held her breath, waiting. *Come on, Solok, put it together. . . .*

Seconds went by in silence. Then the sound of transporter beams filled the bridge, and six columns of light solidified into the forms of a half-dozen armed Vulcans in Starfleet uniforms, standing in front of the view-screen. Solok was among them. His eyes found Kira, who stood in the middle of the bridge, and he raised an eyebrow. "Colonel Kira. Permission to come aboard."

Kira almost laughed. "Granted, Captain. Thanks for dropping in. We could use some help getting the *Gryphon* back under control."

Solok put his people to work with the *Gryphon's* crew, then turned his attention back to Kira. "Captain Mello?" he asked.

"Dead," Kira reported. "Killed by her first officer, who engineered this mess to begin with and who is also dead."

Solok simply nodded. "You took quite a risk, gambling that I would grasp the meaning of your phaser barrage."

"Not really," Kira said evenly. "I had nothing to lose."

"And what would you have done if you had faced a different starship captain?"

Kira arched an eyebrow at him. "I guess we'll never know."

"Indeed," Solok said. "I'm beginning to believe I may have much to learn from further study of manufactured triumphs."

"Good luck with that," Kira replied. "You'll be hard-pressed to find as good a teacher as the one I had."

Twenty-six hours later, with the help of *T'Kumbra*'s engineers, *Gryphon* was restored to full functionality. *Sagittarius* and *Polaris* had recovered all of *Gryphon*'s escape pods with no fatalities, and reunited them with their mothership. Kira bowed out of leading the memorial services for Captain Mello and Commander Montenegro, allowing those of *Gryphon*'s officers who knew them best to eulogize them, while she stood among the crew, mourning as one of many.

When the services were over, Kira returned to the bridge as the ship prepared to get under way for its return voyage to Deep Space 9. Once back at the station, she would relinquish command. This wasn't over by a long shot, she knew. But at least they'd saved Trill.

"Message coming in, Commander," Spillane reported from tactical. "It's from a Trill military transport, approaching us on an intercept course."

Kira looked toward the viewer. "On screen."

The starfield was replaced by the face of large male Trill with white hair and deep frown lines mingling with the dark spots that ran down either side of his face. "Colonel Kira," he began. "I'm General Taulin Cyl of the Trill Defense Ministry. I request permission to come aboard."

Kira's eyes narrowed. "May I assume this is about the assassination of First Minister Shakaar?"

"It's about much more than that, Colonel," General Cyl said. "I'm aware of what you've been through during the past few days. And you deserve to know the truth—you *need* to know the truth, so we can work together to face what's coming."

"Which is what, precisely?" Kira asked.

"The parasites are waging a war, Colonel. And regardless of what you may think, it isn't a war for power. It's a war of revenge."

"Against what?"

"Against the symbionts," Cyl explained. "Humanoids are not the targets of the parasites' war, and we never were. We're the battlefield."

EPILOGUE

"Wormhole in one hour, sir," Bowers said. "Still no response from the station."

"The relay might be malfunctioning," Dax said, standing at Vaughn's shoulder.

Vaughn nodded. "Let's hope that's all it is." Four months ago, in preparation for their mission, *Defiant* and her crew had deployed a subspace relay at the Gamma terminus of the wormhole in order to make communications practical between the Alpha Quadrant and the Gamma Quadrant. During the last few days, however, ever since Vaughn had lifted the comm blackout, there had been no word from the station, and no indication that *Defiant*'s own attempts at communications were being received.

So this is it, Vaughn thought. *I began this mission with such hopes, with so much exuberance, with a*

*ship and crew ready to take on new challenges in the
unknown. Now I end it feeling more battered and
weary than I did before I encountered that Orb in the
Badlands. Why? Why reunite me with my daughter
only so we'd be driven apart? Why guide me here
only to make me face the same choice? Why did
Ruriko have to die again?*

"Captain."

Vaughn turned in the center seat. There was something in Shar's voice that demanded immediate attention. "Ensign?"

"Sir, I'm conducting long-range scans of the space
surrounding the wormhole," Shar began. "I had
thought to determine the status of the relay . . ."

"Yes, Ensign?"

"Captain, the relay is gone."

Shar's words were like a knife in the gut. Before the
Dominion war, the first automated relay that personnel
from Deep Space 9 had deployed in the Gamma Quadrant had been destroyed by the Dominion—a prelude to
the years of conflict that followed. "Was it destroyed?"

"Yes, sir, I believe it was, but—"

"But what, Shar?"

"Sir," Shar said, uncharacteristically flummoxed by
something. "My scans are showing that the space
around the wormhole has been altered since we were
last here."

Everyone turned to look at Shar.

"Altered how?" Dax asked.

"If these readings are correct," Shar said, "the
wormhole now opens within the Idran system."

"Idran?" Vaughn said. Idran was a blue dwarf star of eight uninhabited planets and, Vaughn knew, at a distance of three light-years, was the nearest Gamma Quadrant system to the wormhole. "Are you telling me the wormhole has *moved?*"

"Not at all, sir," Shar said. "The system has."

Vaughn stared at his science officer for a moment, almost ready to accuse Shar of making an exceedingly poor joke. But, of course, Shar seldom joked about anything, and certainly not about something like this.

Vaughn exchanged a look with Dax, who joined Shar at his station to examine the readings herself. "My God," he heard her whisper. "This is unbelievable." Dax looked back at Vaughn. "According to this—"

"Captain!" Bowers said suddenly. "Contact bearing zero-four-zero mark nine. Distance three hundred million kilometers and closing fast. It's a Dominion ship."

"Red alert," Vaughn said at once. "Give me a visual, Mr. Bowers."

On the viewscreen the menacing insectile form of a Jem'Hadar attack ship grew as it approached the *Defiant.*

"Hail them, Sam," Vaughn said.

"Sir, they're hailing us," Bowers said. "And slowing to impulse."

Curiouser and curiouser. "Take us out of warp, Ensign Lankford. Sam . . . on screen."

The Jem'Hadar ship was replaced by a view of its bridge, where a Vorta wearing the monocular headset the Dominion employed in lieu of viewscreens smiled pleasantly at Vaughn. *"Greetings,* Defiant," the Vorta said. *"I trust your little sojourn went well. To whom have I the pleasure of speaking?"*

"I'm Commander Elias Vaughn, captain of this vessel. And you would be . . . ?"

"I'll be damned," Dax muttered, reacting to the Vorta. "Weyoun!"

Weyoun? Vaughn thought. He remembered the name. Weyoun was one of the key figures among the Dominion forces stationed in the Alpha Quadrant during the war.

"Lieutenant Dax," Weyoun beamed, his buttery voice oozing affection. *"How nice it is to see you again."*

"I wish I could return the compliment," Dax said. "I thought the Weyouns were extinct." Like the Jem'Hadar, the Vorta were an engineered species, but one whose members enjoyed a kind of immortality in which memories were recorded and encoded into new clones upon death. At least, as long as the Vorta continued to be useful. Weyoun himself had died several times while in the Alpha Quadrant, only to be replaced by a cloned successor each time. But by all accounts, after the Vorta cloning facilities on Rondac III were destroyed, the last Weyoun had been killed during the final battle on Cardassia.

The Vorta looked positively amused. *"Lieutenant, I was first cloned in the Gamma Quadrant. Did you really think that even if all my clones in the Alpha Quadrant were destroyed, some of my genetic material wasn't still on file in the Dominion?"*

Dax smiled humorlessly. "I might have known it was too much to hope for."

"My dear, you cut me to the quick. Which reminds me . . . how is Commander Worf?"

"He's Ambassador Worf now," Dax said. "To the Klingon Empire."

"Really?" Weyoun said, absently feeling his neck. *"Well, I suppose if anyone would appreciate Mr. Worf's style of discourse, it would be his fellow Klingons."*

"Was there a reason you contacted us, Weyoun?" Vaughn said, trying to get back on topic.

"Oh, my apologies, Commander Vaughn," Weyoun said, and suddenly his voice lost some of his friendliness. *"Our sensors are showing you have a Founder aboard your vessel. We demand his return at once."*

"Of course," Vaughn said, then turned to Dax. "Lieutenant, would you please inform our guest of the situation and arrange to have her beamed aboard the Dominion ship? And be sure to give her the chip." After Dax nodded and left to carry out Vaughn's order, he turned back to Weyoun. "The Founder in question was rescued by us after being marooned for two years on a planet we came across. We were going to bring her with us to Deep Space 9 and then contact the Dominion to arrange her safe return. Your arrival here simplifies that immensely."

"Her?" Weyoun said.

"Yes," Vaughn answered. "She seems quite young—at least, by our standards. Scarcely more than a child. Her ship was brought down two years ago by a force we're quite familiar with—the Borg. She'll attest to what I'm telling you, and she'll also be carrying a report we've compiled about the encounter that you might find useful."

"I see," Weyoun said thoughtfully. He spoke quietly to a nearby Jem'Hadar, similarly equipped with a headset. The soldier nodded and moved off. *Probably the First,* Vaughn thought. *"Yes, we're aware of the Borg from our intelligence on the Alpha Quadrant,"* Weyoun went on. *"Many of us were wondering how long it would be before they paid a visit to the Gamma Quadrant."*

"If you'd like," Vaughn said, "we could perhaps arrange to provide additional intelligence on the Borg as part of an information-exchange pact."

"Thank you for the kind offer, Commander. I'll certainly pass it on to the Founders."

"While we're waiting . . ." Vaughn said, wondering how to phrase his next question, then decided only the direct approach would serve in this situation. "Can you explain what's happened to the Idran system?"

"Oh, yes, Idran," Weyoun said. *"Remarkable, isn't it? And just as I was beginning to believe the universe couldn't become more troublesome. To answer your question, Commander, I cannot begin to explain what's happened here, and I suspect you may find out before I do."*

"But what—" Vaughn started to say when Dax returned to the bridge.

Walking up to the center seat, she reported, "Chao is standing by in the transporter bay."

Vaughn nodded. "Thank you, Lieutenant." He turned back to Weyoun. "Your bridge?"

The Vorta nodded. *"Acceptable."*

"Vaughn to transporter bay," he said. "Chief, please beam the Founder directly to the Dominion ship's bridge."

"Aye, sir. Energizing . . ."

As the Founder materialized near Weyoun, the Vorta bowed his head reverentially and said in a supplicating voice, *"Founder, you honor us with your presence. We're gratified by your safe return. Perhaps you'd care to rest after your ordeal?"*

"Yes, I think I would. Please thank the Federation people for their help to me, and for their hospitality. I owe them my life." With that, she turned and left the bridge of the Dominion ship. For his part, though he clearly was trying not to show it, Weyoun was taken aback by the Founder's words.

"I take it you heard that?" he asked Vaughn.

"Every word," Vaughn confirmed with a small smile. "She's welcome."

"You've done the Dominion a great service, Commander," Weyoun said, *"and you have its gratitude."*

"We could just say you owe us a favor," Vaughn suggested.

"I'd rather not," was Weyoun's cheerful reply. *"But I will say that our meeting this way is fortuitous. You see . . . I believe we've found something that belongs to you."* With a quick nod to someone off

screen, Weyoun turned back to Vaughn and said, *"Safe journey, Commander. Perhaps our paths will cross again someday."* He closed the connection, and disappeared from the viewscreen.

"What the hell was that about?" Vaughn asked aloud.

"Sir," Bowers said. "I'm detecting a transporter beam—"

"Shields!" Vaughn shouted, instantly on his feet.

"Too late—"

Three columns of light shimmered on the bridge and then solidified into the shapes of humanoids: a male and two females. Vaughn didn't recognize any of them, although the male looked human, while one of the females was of a species Vaughn had never seen before. The third member of the group, standing behind the others, was harder to see.

He was about to address them when Dax's voice cut through the bridge. "My God, Jake . . . is that really you?"

Vaughn turned back to the male human, eyes narrowing, knowing Dax could only mean Jake Sisko, son of the former commanding officer of Deep Space 9, missing since before Vaughn's transfer to the station.

Dax ran across the bridge and launched herself at the tall young man, having to jump up to throw her arms around his neck.

"Woah, Ezri, take it easy," Jake said, laughing.

"You big jerk," she said. "Kasidy and your grandfather have been worried sick about you. We all have."

"I know," Jake said quietly, holding her close. "I'm sorry. Nothing worked out the way I expected."

"Sir," Bowers said to Vaughn. "The Dominion ship is moving off."

"Stand down from red alert, Mr. Bowers," Vaughn said, "and have Dr. Bashir report to the bridge." He paused, trying to recall what he knew about young Mr. Sisko, then added with a smile, "Get Nog up here as well."

Dax detached himself from the lad. "Where have you been?" Dax demanded of Jake, and as he opened his mouth to answer, she added, "And if you're even thinking about saying 'It's a long story,' you better think twice, or so help me—"

"Later," Jake said. "I promise I'll explain everything, but not now. Not yet." Jake turned and focused on Vaughn. He smiled, but it was wistful. "It's so weird to see someone else in charge here," he said, then caught himself. "I'm sorry, Commander. I'm Jake Sisko. I've been away for a while. Permission to come aboard?"

Vaughn smiled. *I like this young man already.* "No apology necessary, Mr. Sisko. Permission granted. I'm Elias Vaughn. Welcome aboard, to you and your companions. . . ."

As if realizing the oversight, Jake hastily corrected it. "Oh, God, I'm sorry. I forgot to introduce my new friends. This is Wex," he said, indicating the first female. She had gray skin and an impressive mane of white hair. "She's on a pilgrimage," Jake explained.

Wex inclined her head but said nothing as she regarded Vaughn, seeming to scrutinize him.

"And, uh, this is my other new friend—which I

suppose is kind of ironic, all things considering," Jake continued, indicating the woman who still hung back. She stepped forward, her stout frame wrapped in worn, weathered cloaks. She pulled back her hood and revealed a head of close-cropped silver hair. And judging from the ridges of her nose, she was unmistakably Bajoran. Vaughn heard a sharp intake of breath from Dax.

"I apologize for the condition in which I greet you, Commander," she said humbly, spreading her hands. Her voice, Vaughn thought, was soft and seemed to convey the impression of wisdom—ancient wisdom, of a kind he himself had long searched for but never found. "Permit me to express my gratitude for your timely assistance. I am Opaka, once kai of Bajor."

THE DEEP SPACE NINE SAGA
CONTINUES IN
RISING SON

Look for STAR TREK fiction from Pocket Books

Star Trek®

Star Trek®: The Original Series

Star Trek: The Next Generation®

Star Trek: Voyager®

Star Trek®: Stargazer

Star Trek®: Starfleet Corps of Engineers (eBooks)

#2 • *Chainmail* • Diane Carey
#3 • *Doors Into Chaos* • Robert Greenberger
#4 • *Demons of Air and Darkness* • Keith R.A. DeCandido
#5 • *No Man's Land* • Christie Golden
#6 • *Cold Wars* • Peter David
#7 • *What Lay Beyond* • various
Epilogue: Here There Be Monsters • Keith R.A. DeCandido

Star Trek®: The Badlands

#1 • Susan Wright
#2 • Susan Wright

Star Trek®: Dark Passions

#1 • Susan Wright
#2 • Susan Wright

Star Trek® Omnibus Editions

Invasion! Omnibus • various
Day of Honor Omnibus • various
The Captain's Table Omnibus • various
Star Trek: Odyssey • William Shatner with Judith and Garfield Reeves-Stevens
Millennium Omnibus • Judith and Garfield Reeves-Stevens
Starfleet: Year One • Michael Jan Friedman

Other Star Trek® Fiction

Legends of the Ferengi • Ira Steven Behr & Robert Hewitt Wolfe
Strange New Worlds, vol. I, II, III, IV, and V • Dean Wesley Smith, ed.
Adventures in Time and Space • Mary P. Taylor, ed.
Captain Proton: Defender of the Earth • D.W. "Prof" Smith
New Worlds, New Civilizations • Michael Jan Friedman
The Lives of Dax • Marco Palmieri, ed.
The Klingon Hamlet • Wil'yam Shex'pir
Enterprise Logs • Carol Greenburg, ed.
Amazing Stories • various

Picard comes face to face with a man
who may be his most dangerous
adversary yet...
and a surprisingly personal nemesis.

STAR TREK
nemesis

novelization by
J. M. Dillard

story by
John Logan & Rick Berman
& Brent Spiner

screenplay by
John Logan

Star Trek® created by Gene Roddenberry

THIS NOVEMBER!

STAR TREK®
THE STARFLEET SURVIVAL GUIDE